REBEL DRAGON

THE DRAGONS OF ESTERNES, BOOK 1

STEVE TURNBULL

TAU PRESS LTD

1

The floorboards trembled beneath her and she came awake with a jump.

The air in the eyrie was cold against her skin, and the light of the smaller moon, Colimar, shone red through the arched window in the tower's stone wall. It was still deepest night.

Must have been a dream, thought Kantees, as she re-adjusted the thin blanket and tried to burrow deeper into the pricking straw. The boards beneath her shifted again and there was a quiet grumble. *Oh, by the Mother's milk. What now? Stupid animal.*

She contemplated doing nothing, pretending not to wake up. Maybe Sheesha would lose interest and go back to sleep. The boards jumped again and Kantees groaned.

"Go back to sleep, Sheesha, it's not even close to morning," she hissed through the cracks. There was nothing to see since the gaps were smaller than her finger-width and there was no light down there anyway. Her reward was to have the boards bumped three more times. Sheesha must be stretching.

While Sheesha might be an animal, he was cleverer than most, even those of his own species. But that didn't stop him behaving like a spoilt child, like little Jelamie, the mistress's youngest. He was always getting into things and places he shouldn't.

Sheesha snuffled at her. The noise he made when he wanted something. Perhaps he'd spilt his water bucket again. He was forever doing that with his tail; it was like he didn't even know he had it.

Maybe it was important. What if Sheesha was ill? If there was a problem with her charge and Kantees ignored it, there'd be trouble.

"And," she said, "if there's nothing wrong, I'll make trouble for *you*."

Kantees climbed to her feet. Her eyes were adjusted to the dark and she could see the mounds of straw and the dark shadow that was the path through them. The hole in the floor to the lower level was a black pit. She picked up the gauntlets and slipped her fingers into the soft leather, then donned the protective hat. Sheesha had never attacked her but it was better to be safe than sorry. The *zirichak* had never woken her in the night either.

Before he had learnt to fly, Sheesha had been very demanding and very annoying. Kantees was glad those days were long past and, what with Sheesha and Jelamie, had decided she was never going to have any children. Even if the master chose someone for her to marry.

Not bothering with the stairs, Kantees grabbed the rope, swung out, wrapped her legs around it and slid to the next level. After all these years she barely noticed the smell—she would be mucking out in the morning—but was almost knocked over when Sheesha rattled over and nudged her in the shoulder. He was almost twice her height

Automatically Kantees reached up and scratched beneath the feathers in the place Sheesha liked the most.

Sheesha pulled back. In the dim light the *zirichak* waddled back—he was far more elegant in the air—brought his hook-beaked head down to Kantees and, with one eye, stared at her.

Kantees had no idea what he wanted. This behaviour was completely new.

"What?" hissed Kantees, as if Sheesha could understand, which was ridiculous because *ziri* were just animals, to be raced by the masters.

Her train of thought was interrupted by the distant sound of an arrow. It was only a momentary whine; it ended with a thump.

Sheesha turned his head and lifted it as if he were looking out of the window.

Taking care not to trip on the hobble chain that prevented Sheesha trying to fly inside, Kantees hurried across to the open hatch. She stuck her head out into a freezing breeze. Squinting, she tried to see.

With only Colimar in the sky, lying close to the horizon, the shadows were long and deep. But at least the sky was clear—if it hadn't been she would have been able to see nothing. As it was, she could make out the shapes of the buildings—she was familiar with them, anyway—but hanging in the air near the wall was something huge like a growth.

She shook her head and looked again. Was she still dreaming? A great bulbous shape, where the light caught it there were bumps and lines that looked, for all the world, like leaves. But leaves as big as a house. It couldn't be a *tekrak*; they never grew that big. But her eyes said it was.

And hanging beneath it, some sort of construction that was hard to make out. And from that, shadowy human shapes were jumping onto the main wall.

An attack?

Sheesha bumped her in the middle of her back, knocking her forwards onto the deep windowsill.

Kantees turned and stroked the huge head, and made settling noises. "It's all right, nothing to worry about."

Nothing for us to worry about. They were heading into the main building. It was nothing to do with her. If the masters wanted to fight, why should she care?

She stared out once more at the massive *tekrak* poised above the wall. No family she knew of had such things. Even now she could scarce believe what she was seeing. Could the *Slissac* have returned to put all the Taymalin to the sword?

The master and mistress, Lord and Lady Jakalain, were decent people even if they had no idea how to bring up children, nor did they treat the slaves badly. Every one of the Kadralin knew how lucky they were, they knew the stories about families that punished their slaves for the slightest crime, and even killed them for pleasure. Kantees enjoyed her life looking after Sheesha and some of the other *zirichasa*. If the Jakalain were killed, what would happen to her? What would happen to Sheesha?

Perhaps the castle would be taken over by another family who would not be decent.

Mother's milk.

But what could she do? She was here in the Ziri Tower, and by the time she got to ground level and across to the other side it would all be over—and she might well run into a raider. Then she would be dead.

Sheesha prodded her in the back again.

Kantees turned round slowly. She knew Sheesha was intelligent, at least for a *zirichak*, but he couldn't possibly understand what was happening. Surely he did not want Kantees to ride him? For a start, that was a hanging offence and Kantees was quite fond of her life. That also meant Kantees had never flown, although she knew all the equipment and had sat in the saddle holding the reins. Never mind she was a slave.

She looked out of the window again to see more men on the wall now.

But she dared not—it could mean her life. It wasn't fair. Why couldn't someone else make the decision? Why hadn't any of the other *zirichasa* noticed? Why hadn't any armsmen seen what was happening? That was their job.

Because they're dead.

Kantees let out a cry of angry frustration. She turned and pushed Sheesha's head out of the way as she half ran to the tack room. It was too dark to see but she had everything in its correct place and knew where to find the lightest practice saddle.

Sheesha was crouched and waiting with his head down for her to slip the bridle over.

It took a couple of minutes to get the saddle in position and strapped firmly. What a laugh it would be if she took off and then slipped and fell to smash her head open on the rocks. Ha.

The one thing she didn't have was a flying suit. Why would she? There would be almost nothing between her and the freezing air. If she didn't fall, she would probably die of the cold. At least the protective hat would help keep her head warm.

Pulling the last strap tight, she paused. Sheesha dipped his chest so his wings were folded high above them, his claws scratching on the boards. Kantees went to the wall and unhooked the chain that ran from there through the metal collar to the cuffs on his feet. She was a little nervous. He was acting so strangely. There were tales of *zirichak* killing their keepers, but that had never happened here as far as she knew. Those keepers probably had mistreated their charges.

The chain rattled as it went through the cuff. There still hadn't been any noise from outside. What was she going to do when she got out there? She had never been in the main parts of the castle—except the kitchens. She did not know her way around.

For the hundredth time, it seemed, she wondered what she was doing.

Then it occurred to her. Why hadn't the warning bell sounded? It was mounted on one of the side towers and would wake everyone. She opened the great doors that were big enough to let Sheesha fly, then went back to him. She could see by the way he kept dipping his head he was impatient.

She was about to commit a capital crime. She would be hanged for it.

Sheesha squawked and shuffled in his crouched, cramped position. Perhaps she could claim, in her defence, that Sheesha had demanded she ride him. Somehow she did not think that would be very convincing.

She slipped her right foot into the stirrup and brought her left leg up and over. The straps were too long so she shortened them so she could rest her feet firmly. She sat awkwardly and grabbed for the belt that held the rider in position. Sheesha edged towards the door, his great wings moving forwards to hold up his body. Kantees grabbed the reins and pulled them back, not too tight but just taking up the slack along Sheesha's sinuous, feathered neck.

It was then she remembered he always gave a loud trumpet whenever he launched himself into the air. Announcing his emergence into the world, like a challenge.

The attackers would know and they would shoot their arrows, at the very least they would hit Sheesha and that would be enough to kill him.

Sheesha reached the edge and raised his clawed wings to hook them into the frame above the opening. His head poked out and she could see him surveying the air.

Then she was flung back as he dropped into the dark. She tried not to yank on the reins, which were only for guidance. A *zirichak* knew how to fly; the rider only needed to direct the creature left and right, up and down.

Sheesha's wings flicked out but he was diving. All she could see was the small courtyard between the Ziri Tower and the main building. There was a man standing there. He carried an unsheathed sword but she could only see the top of his head.

Could Sheesha tell friends from enemies? Kantees knew he had a sense of smell but how good was it? And another thing, she had been given to understand that *zirichasa* did not fly at night. That was the wisdom passed to her from old Romain. Perhaps he was wrong.

The freezing air shot through her clothes as if they were not even there.

The ground was coming at them. She knew he would pull up. She prayed to the Mother he would pull up. Perhaps they didn't fly at night because they crashed into the ground.

Something changed and her weight was forced into the saddle. The world tilted up slightly and Sheesha passed across the outside wall, still going down but now at a flatter angle. All right, he could fly at night.

They were in shadow now. The castle was built atop one of the foothills that encircled the great mountains that made up the heart of Esternes.

Sheesha was flying level now, the wall of the castle beside them. Every now and then she saw the light of a torch or lamp in the interior through the arrow slits. Then they were past and out into moonlight again, flashing across the scrubland that was only useful for grazing animals.

Where was he going? They needed to do something at the castle … but what?

Gingerly she pulled on the right rein. The response from Sheesha was instantaneous as he banked giddily and the world turned. And there was the rear of the castle, with its walls as high and impregnable as the rest.

Walls easily breached by men aboard a *tekrak* of such enormous size it could carry them in a basket beneath. She shook her head. She had never heard of such a thing.

She focused on the towers. They had already passed the bell tower once on the flight out. It was not as high as the main tower, and it was narrow. With gentle tugs she steered Sheesha to ensure he would fly back the way he had come. She did not want to be on the other side, where the *tekrak* hung.

How could she make him gain height? They were flying only a few feet above the ground. She pulled the reins again and leaned back. Up to now Sheesha had barely flapped his wings. She knew from Romain the wild *zirichasa* soared on the air currents in the mountains and could glide all day without a single beat of their wings if the winds were with them.

But now Sheesha's powerful wings stroked hard and with each downbeat he rose and she was pushed down into the saddle. She was not sure of the best way to approach the tower. It would be best if she was not seen, since she had no desire to become a pincushion for arrows. But the tower itself went high above the level of the walls and Sheesha could not climb vertically. She pulled on his right rein again and leaned forwards. He banked right and flew directly away from the castle.

Kantees looked back over her shoulder. The dark silhouette of the castle with the *tekrak* like a bulbous growth was highlighted against the dull red light of Colimar. She was desperately cold but had to keep going.

She pulled hard on the left rein and Sheesha almost turned over as he banked left. The ground was a long way away. Kantees urged him forwards, goading him with her heels and words. He beat faster and they sped up; she pulled back and he climbed. She judged they were on exactly the right course for the top of the tower.

Kantees reached with her numb fingers for the belt buckle.

They came up over the top of the bell tower from below. Kantees threw her weight forwards and Sheesha almost fell out of the sky to land on the roof, hind legs first, pulling in his wings to act as his front legs.

Then someone said, "Oi!"

2

Kantees almost fell out of the saddle and ended up on her hands and knees. She had not realised how cold she was—or how much warmth she had been taking from Sheesha's body. The muscles in her legs ached from the unaccustomed strain, and her inner thighs were rubbed raw.

She hadn't even noticed while they'd been in the air.

"Who are you?"

She lifted her head and, looking under Sheesha's neck, could see a man's legs. He was only a short distance away but probably nervous of the *zirichak*.

"You with the Dunor?"

She wasn't going to say she wasn't. She reached out, grabbed a handful of Sheesha's feathers and pulled herself to her feet. It was dark, and as long as she stayed on this side of Sheesha's neck the man wouldn't be able to tell who she was.

The bell stood in its frame only a short distance away. Next to it lay a body. The longer she delayed, the more likely people would be killed.

"Of course." She tried to give her voice a deeper sound, as if she were a messenger. Not that messengers rode fine beasts like Sheesha, nobody rode the *ziri* except racers, but perhaps he wasn't an expert.

No, he'd been relegated to guarding the bell tower. No use for anything else. Though she was not sure how he could have got up here undetected.

That he had done so was enough for her. She took hold of the reins and walked across the roof, keeping Sheesha between them.

"What's the message then, boy?"

"The message?"

She had covered a third of the distance. Sheesha's wings scraped the roof as he moved beside her, taking much smaller strides than he was used to.

"Stop," he said.

She stopped. What could she do? She was no fighter and even if she was she had no weapon. And no armour—barely any clothes at all. Her teeth were chattering. Trying to be clever was just not working and the cold was biting through her skin. Her very dark skin.

"Kadralin slave!"

She dropped the reins and ran for the bell. She did not know how long it would take him to react, or whether he had any throwing weapons. Or worse, a bow.

There had been no rain for a few days but there was plenty of frost on the roof. She was only a couple of paces from the bell when her left foot flew out from under her and she pitched forwards.

The thudding of his heavy feet pounded closer. She turned to see him with his sword raised above his head. It came down. Instinctively she rolled towards him. The blow landed where she had been as she impacted with his legs; it knocked the wind from her and she cried out in pain. He went flying as he tripped over her and his head smashed into the bell. It rang out with a sonorous gong that bounced off the towers and echoed through the courtyard below. Ignoring her screaming ribs, she got to her feet and found the metal striker in a bucket at the side.

She hit the bell again and again.

The soldier pushed himself up, so she hit him as well, whacking his temple with the striker's bulbous head. He let out a groan of pain and slumped back. She trod on his hand and returned to bashing the bell with all her strength.

Sheesha snapped his beak in displeasure at the noise.

"Big strong *ziri* like you? It's only a bit of noise!" shouted Kantees with a laugh. She moved the striker further down the bell and the noise became deeper and louder. She turned to look at the main tower. Lights were being lit and showing at the window. Silhouetted figures stood for a moment looking out and then disappeared fast back inside. She hoped they were readying themselves for battle.

The *tekrak* was big—no, it was huge—but she guessed its complement of soldiers could not be more than thirty at most. And there were many times that number of armsmen in the castle. The attackers could only prevail by stealth, and they no longer had that advantage.

A horn winded from the far side of the castle walls. Torches were being lit inside the huge basket hanging from the *tekrak*. It had windows just like the castle.

Men streamed back along the walls. They were retreating.

The one at her feet tried to crawl away.

"Sheesha! Come!" she called and the *zirichak* thumped and scraped his way over. Long ago, Romain had drawn the bones of the creature for her so she could learn them by heart. Their wings were like hands but with one less finger and much bigger and spread out. When they walked it was as if they were on their elbows with their forearms and fingers pointing upwards. It wasn't elegant.

They had back legs, of course, and sometimes they went up on those alone—usually when threatening or mating.

"If you try to run away, I will let Sheesha eat you," she said and the man froze on the ground. She stopped banging the bell, having succeeded in what she was attempting, and went to Sheesha, walking him closer to the prone guard.

"Throw your sword away," she commanded.

He gripped it tighter.

"Sheesha, speak!"

And the *zirichak* let out an intense squawk, which was a version of the sound he used when complaining but the guard didn't know that. It wasn't Kantees' fault that, despite being told not to teach Sheesha tricks, he learnt things very quickly.

The sword skittered across the roof.

"And your knife."

It went in the other direction.

There was a thunderous roar from across the castle and the Zirichak Tower was lit almost like daylight. The *tekrak* had started its burn. Of course she had seen the swarms of *tekrasa* crossing the skies in spring and autumn. Usually they were mere dots, so high did they float, but at night they descended to earth and their roots dug into the soil so they could feed.

In places where crops grew, the farmers and villagers would come out into the fields to destroy them. Each *tekrak* had a tube at one end, effectively the rear, and they propelled themselves by generating a fire that shot out. It was their magic. They had to be killed because their fire could burn the crops.

The ones that landed in the castle couldn't root anyway, and they were easy to get rid of. But when they took off in the morning the roots came up, their bodies—now bloated with gas—lifted them into the sky, and their fire-tubes drove them away in their swarm.

But this *tekrak* had a fire-tube that shot a flame almost the length of the protective wall. It moved with incredible slowness, a leviathan of the air.

Kantees turned her attention back to the guard. "I want your cloak."

His hands fumbled at his neck.

Sheesha pulled at the reins and shrieked at the *tekrak* as it floated across the courtyard, ropes dangling from the basket. She could even see inside. A man, in the robes of a patterner, sat in the front concentrating. His eyes were closed. Soldiers looked back at her and one barked orders.

The *tekrak* accelerated. Sheesha dragged her up as he rose on his hind legs and beat his wings, threatening the monstrous plant.

"No, Sheesha!" she called at him but he wasn't listening. She clung to the reins. Romain had told her a *zirichak* could not go aloft if someone held the reins. So she clung to them swinging and twisting as Sheesha pulled her off her feet.

The *tekrak* filled the sky and roared overhead. She saw a door open in the side of the basket from which a man with a bow leaned out. The roaring of the massive fire-tube drowned out all other sound. But when she saw him loose three arrows in quick succession, she was terrified he was aiming for her or, even worse, at Sheesha. Then the *tekrak* went over them. And she felt no pain, while Sheesha continued to screech his defiance at the monster.

Heat and flame roared across them. Sheesha squealed and curled up into a tight ball. Kantees thudded to the ground and rolled over.

The wash of heat was gone almost as quickly as it arrived but it left behind a disgusting stench that made the bile rise in her throat. The flame tube lit the top of the tower with its eerie blue light. Raising her head she saw the three arrows, planted in the body of the man she had overpowered.

They could not stop for him, but they would not let him remain alive to reveal any secrets. Hard-hearted as it seemed, she understood the logic.

Kantees went to Sheesha and flung her arms around him, burying herself in his feathers. It was partly to comfort him and give him something familiar. But it also meant she could keep warm, since she did not desire to wrap herself in a cloak now wet with blood.

As she clung to his warmth, a cold certainty crept through her. She was in trouble.

It was true she had saved the castle, they would not be able to deny it, but the fact remained she had ridden Sheesha. And the law was the law. There were so many stories where slaves had done something wrong in an attempt to do the right thing and were punished regardless of the balance.

She had ridden a *zirichak* in defiance of the law. The punishment was death.

But what if they never found out?

The castle was coming alive. Sounds of shouts and arguments floated up from the courtyard. There were armsmen moving on the walls opposite. She did not know if she had been seen but perhaps if she could get Sheesha back into his eyrie they might get away with it.

The trapdoor rattled. Even Sheesha jumped.

"Sheesha, come on," she said and grabbed the reins. With the excitement over, he moved without haste. She yanked at the reins to make him move faster. It didn't work. Once he reached the outside edge of the tower she mounted and dug her heels in.

He spread his wings, hopped up onto the wall, and dropped over the side. This time she was ready for it, and happy since it took them out of sight instantly.

The ground rushed at them. She allowed Sheesha his head and, barely a man's height from the ground, he snapped his wings out into horizontal flight, careening across the ground.

The entrance to Sheesha's eyrie faced the courtyard but if they came in fast from the far side they might not be seen. As she arched him away to the south, she glanced to see if the *tekrak* was still in view but she saw nothing. The bright glow in the sky could just as easily be another star while the false dawn of Lostimal, the second, larger moon, glowed on the horizon. Unlike the dull red of Colimar, Lostimal was white.

She turned to look ahead. The town of Beedun's Ford had already passed behind them, she was not concerned about that. The town would be asleep at this time and would know nothing of the fight at the castle.

Just as she had done before, she brought Sheesha round in a tight turn and headed him back towards the castle. As Lostimal rose, this side of the structure was bathed in its white light, which was inconvenient but unavoidable.

She had been into the town during feast days and the times when she had gone to fetch for the masters, and had thought it was big. Somehow, from the back of a *zirichak* it did not seem quite so large. The Beedun ran through it, splitting off the miners' quarter from the rest. The river was milky—the colour it had as it flowed from the mountains—but now it looked red like blood, reflecting the light of Colimar, though Lostimal would soon take over.

The old ford was in the north, but bridges spanned the river now and was only used by the miners' wagons because either the bridges were too narrow or the cargo too heavy.

And then she was past it and following the rising land. Sheesha beat his wings in deep powerful strokes. She pulled back more and Sheesha gained even more height. The Ziri Tower was coming at her. She knew the height of the eyrie; she thought she even recognised her window. She pulled Sheesha to the left to stay in shadow and out of the light of Lostimal, at least until the last moment.

Which arrived in the blink of an eye.

As she turned Sheesha round the curve of the tower she came into full view of every person on the walls and in the courtyard. She prayed to the Mother no one would look up at exactly that moment.

Sheesha did not require guidance now. Although he entered the eyrie at a sharper angle than usual and came to a crashing halt inside, thumping into the bales of hay. The hay wasn't for eating since *zirichasa* ate meat, but provided warmth and something to sleep on, like a nest the wild animals would make for themselves.

Kantees unbuckled herself from the seat and slid to the ground. Her legs gave way again and she was freezing but she forced herself to the eyrie doors and closed them. She could not decide whether fast or slow was better. Fast because it got them shut, or slow because they would not attract attention.

Sheesha was already curled up into a tight ball and probably asleep. His breathing was unhurried. More than could be said for hers.

Was that real? Had she really just ridden Sheesha across the sky and saved the castle? It was like being a hero from a story. Except she would be a hero strung up on a gibbet if anyone else knew what she had done. Although that was a very sobering thought, the excitement refused to leave her. And so did the cold.

It was also forbidden to sleep with the *zirichasa*. One reason was that they might decide to eat you in the night. She had never heard of that happening except in Romain's stories. The other reason—probably the real one, she now realised—was that they did not want any *zirichak* to form too strong a bond with their keepers, who were always slaves. And a slave might get it into their head that they could ride.

And she had. She had not fallen off.

"Kadralin cannot fly," Romain had said. "We do not have the skill, and we do not have the command. That is why we are slaves and the Taymalin are the masters."

Not true. She had flown and she had survived—and she had loved it.

She shivered and looked at the compact form of Sheesha. What did it matter if he ate her? After all, in the morning she might be arrested and hanged. Why avoid one risk of death when another was just as likely?

She walked over to Sheesha and petted his neck, saying his name quietly. She leaned her weight on him and as he moved slightly, a space opened up under a wing and she pushed into it. With her head against his chest, hearing his breathing and feeling his powerful heart, she closed her eyes. His wing dropped down to cover her and she slept in his warmth.

3

The next morning the castle was in uproar. From the eyrie, Kantees could hear all the shouting and the arguments. Armsmen marched down to the town. The house patterner, with a retinue, was sent to the Jakalain Circle so that he could send messages.

After tending to Sheesha, who was tired and irritable—just as she was—Kantees descended to the kitchen in the base of the tower. No one looked at her in any way other than the usual. But there seemed no time for talk.

Libbibet, a middle-aged Kadralin woman who ran the servants' kitchen below the tower, was serving as usual and put a couple of spoonfuls of porridge into Kantees' bowl. But instead of her usual expression of merriment and a kind word, her face was serious and her lips pressed together in concerned silence.

Kantees had already decided—after discussing it with the irritable Sheesha, who had failed to offer any advice—that she would pretend she knew nothing. She did not think anyone would have recognised Sheesha in the dark anyway. Even with the light of Lostimal, it only seemed bright because it had been so dark before.

"What's the fuss?" said Kantees.

Libbibet paused, her hand poised with the third spoonful hanging over Kantees' bowl. She glanced around as if she did not wish to be overheard.

"Lord Jelamie has been stolen away," she hissed. "Raiders in the night."

Kantees was as shocked as the woman. Jelamie was barely seven. He might be a precocious little tyrant, but to be taken from one's family by force? Kantees was doubly shocked because she had seen what had happened, though she did not remember seeing anyone carrying a child.

But she could say nothing.

"Why would someone do that?"

Libbibet leaned forwards conspiratorially. "They say it was the *Slissac* returned."

Kantees had to fight back the words of denial that threatened to burst from her. It had not been the mythical lizard people. She knew it was just the Taymalin. But she could tell no one.

"I wouldn't believe that," she said. "Whenever anything bad happens it's always the *Slissac* that are blamed and no one has seen one for a thousand years or more."

"Children get stolen away in the night by them," said Libbibet. "For their monstrous patterns and ceremonies."

Kantees just shook her head and looked down at the spoon still suspended above her bowl. "Can I have that, then?"

Libbibet slopped it down. "You may scoff all you like." And then she went off into the Kadralin tongue, which Kantees had never learnt because she had been bred and born in slavery and use of the Kadralin tongue would earn any slave a lashing.

Kantees moved away and went to one of the benches reserved for the keepers. Old Romain was there, as was Galiko, who helped look after the older *zirichasa* that no longer flew races. He was simple but had a good heart.

"Where are the others?" she asked as she sat on the bench and put down her bowl.

"Called to the grand hall," said Romain. "To be interrogated until they reveal the truth."

Kantees hid her nervousness with a spoonful of porridge.

"Am I not to go?" she said, thinking that with the house patterner gone off to the ley-circle, she would not be subject to any magic that might force her to betray the truth.

"Later," was all Romain said.

She nodded and applied herself to her breakfast to avoid further conversation.

"The race in the next ten-day has been cancelled," said Romain. "Sheesha will not be required."

"Is it true Jelamie has been stolen away, as Libbibet says?" she asked.

"It is true," said Romain. "The Lady is distraught and has taken to her rooms. The master is in a dangerous mood and it would not do to cross him."

"Look, Sheesha crapping in the middle of the parade of winners wasn't my fault."

"You embarrassed our masters," said Romain.

She knew better than to talk back but she didn't think a *zirichak* doing its business in a parade was on the same level as having one's child stolen away. No matter how embarrassing it might have been at the time. And she had been punished, although not even Romain with all his experience had any guidance to offer on how to stop an excited animal pooing in public, even if it did offend the sensibilities of some of the more elite of the masters.

Kantees certainly didn't blame Sheesha. He had just come second in an important race and he was excited.

"And they came in the night?"

"Riding a monstrous *tekrak* by all accounts," said Romain.

"Flyer beaten by a flyer," said Galiko. It was barely more than a mutter but Kantees heard it and stared at him. Galiko went on eating his porridge using a tiny spoon he kept with him. He would not use one of the big spoons so it always took him a long time, but no one got angry.

"Why was I not called with the other keepers?" she said to Romain.

"They sleep together. You are separate."

They were all male and had a dormitory off the eyries of the yearlings. She cared for the only racer the Jakalain had; there would be no more unless they bought in new stock or until the yearlings matured. And she was a girl.

The Jakalain had only begun to keep racing *zirichasa* at the request of the heir, their much older son, Daybian. The tower had been there but unused. The boy who had been stolen away, Jelamie, was just the spare to inherit, in case something happened to his elder brother.

"You should present yourself at the hall before midday," said Romain as he got up. He glanced over at Galiko, as he always did, and sighed at the boy's slowness. "Gally!"

The boy beamed. "Romain, sir."

Kantees felt it was impossible to be angry with such innocence, though Romain often was.

"We must winch new hay to the old ones," said Romain, speaking loudly and slowly as if Galiko were deaf and stupid. "Hurry up and finish."

"Yes, Romain."

Galiko went back to his porridge and took another slow spoonful.

The stool Kantees was sitting on scraped as she pushed it back and moved across to sit opposite Galiko.

"What did you mean about a flyer beating a flyer?"

"Gally is stupid. And Gally is slow," said Galiko not looking up from his own food. He took another small mouthful, sucking the spoon clean.

"No, you're not," she said. "Gally is clever and Gally is quiet. And"—she glanced around to make sure no one was close—"if Gally saw anything last night that might get someone into trouble then he has to keep his mouth shut."

His gaze flicked up to meet hers for a moment and then slid away.

"Gally, please," she said quietly. "If you tell them, they will hang me."

He frowned into his porridge. "Kill Kantees?"

"Yes, kill me."

He sat up and put his hand on hers and squeezed it. "Don't want Kantees killed."

"Neither do I."

He grinned at that. "Gally keeps secrets," he said. "Gally keeps lots of secrets."

"Really?" she said. "Like what?"

"Romain loves Kantees," he said.

She imagined, for a brief moment, kissing the face of the old man, laughed, and then realised this was not the time and turned it into a cough.

"Yes, well, Gally," she said. "That's a secret you can keep to the end of time because it's certainly not true."

He squeezed her hand and nodded.

"Never mind, I shouldn't have asked because then it's not a secret." She hesitated. "So, if someone asks about last night and my secret, you won't tell them, will you?"

He shook his head and let go of her hand.

"Promise me, Gally."

"Gally promises, Kantees."

She tried to delay going to the grand hall. Even though she knew it would be better to get it over with. It was like having a splinter, it was uncomfortable but the thought of taking it out was so much worse.

Instead she went back to the eyrie and worked hard doing the chores she had been putting off for many a five-day. Tidying the riding gear, putting aside those items that needed repair. Reorganising the hay bales—exhausting work that made her sweat despite the cold wind blowing through.

But there came a point when it could not be delayed any longer— because otherwise it would be past midday instead of before, then she would have disobeyed, and with that would come punishment. And, quite possibly, the assumption that she was either guilty or knew something.

She gave Sheesha a pat on the neck and he offered the place under his chin for her to scratch. She gave it a little rub, just to show she cared, and then headed for the ladder. The eyrie itself, unlike her loft, had stone slabs for a floor. *Zirichasa* did not like wooden floors. Kantees guessed this was because they nested on the ground. They were big enough that they would have few enemies to worry about.

The ladder went through a small hole in the stone. On the far side was a walled-off area with a wooden trapdoor through which the hay bales were lifted. She had heard the doors crashing shut as each bale went up to the higher eyrie where Romain and Gally worked.

She arrived at the kitchen level and set off towards the main part of the castle. She had been there so rarely it made her nervous.

The guards on the inner gate were more alert than usual, though it was clearly a case of closing the cage after the bird had flown. But they didn't know that. She even heard people calling Jelamie's name. And it looked as if they had sent someone down into the well. After all, it was possible he had just wandered off. It wouldn't have been the first time.

But as Kantees crossed the wide courtyard she glanced up at the wall where the *tekrak* had been tethered. Its fire had blackened the stone of the building with a great soot stain. She glanced up at the bell tower but there was nothing to be seen. They would have found the man with the three arrows in his body.

Someone had rung the bell to warn the castle. One might think it was him and he had been silenced by the arrows. But then it would be realised that he was not a member of the household, and the real guard was there too. Perhaps they would attribute the bell ringing to the original guard, though that made little sense.

No one would imagine that a slave had, in defiance of the law, ridden a *zirichak* to ring the bell and warn the castle.

She started to go down some steps to a small door. Since she was no more than a slave, the idea of going through the main entrance did not even cross her mind.

"Wait," said an armsman. She did not recognise him, but there was no reason why she should. Her life was secluded.

"Sir?"

"What's your name?"

"Kantees, sir." She gestured in the direction of the tower.

"The keeper of Sheesha?"

"Yes, sir."

"Come with me. You're late."

She hesitated for a moment but returned to the courtyard. He waited for her and then headed in through the main door. She stopped before it.

"Sir?"

He turned. "Stop wasting my time and come along."

She swallowed, this was another rule. Not punishable by death but a whipping certainly. The fact that she had been told to do it by someone in authority did not make it any easier. Her early life had been a game of ensuring no rules were broken so that she was not punished. And of protecting others if she could, even if it meant she would be punished instead.

Then again, she had broken so many rules now, what difference did this one make?

She followed her escort. He did not go to the main hall, though she could see its massive grandeur of pillars and balconies through open doors as she passed. As far as she could tell they went the full length of a passage that ran along the hall and then turned right along another one where doors led off into smaller rooms.

Finally the armsman deposited her in a room with huge windows that looked out towards the mountains. Jakalain was a lonely place on the edge of the wilderness. The heart of the island of Esternes was massive peaks and deep valleys where the wild *zirichasa*, as well as other creatures she knew nothing of, flew free. At least, that's what she'd heard.

There was no one else in the room. Behind a table of dark wood stood three chairs, and on its surface lay writing implements—being a slave she could neither read nor write.

There was another chair facing the table.

"Sit there," said the armsman.

"Sit?"

"When the lord enters, you stand up. After he and anyone else with him has sat down, you can sit."

"I'd rather stand."

"You will sit."

He sounded tired. But he had probably been up all night.

"Is there any knowledge of the lordling?" she asked.

His eyes narrowed. "What do you know of it?"

She was terrified her guilt stood out on her face. "Nothing, just gossip in the kitchen."

"Keep your gossip to yourself."

With that he left her alone in the room with the chair that had both a padded seat and a padded back. It looked comfortable but she could not bring herself to sit in it. She had been working in the eyrie and had not cleaned herself up. She was probably soiling the rugs on which she stood; she certainly did not want to dirty the beautiful chair.

Being alone and waiting was terrifying. She felt her heart pounding and she sweated—though that could have been from her earlier exertions. She probably stank, and cursed herself for being so stupid as to engage in hard manual labour before meeting with such important people. But perhaps they expected her to stink.

The armsman had implied that Lord Jakalain himself would be here. It was true that she was often in close proximity to the lords, because she was usually in attendance with Sheesha. But they never spoke to her.

She closed her eyes as a door in the wall beyond the table opened.

4

She gripped the back of the chair with one hand as three men entered. She realised her other hand was shaking and shoved it behind her back. Her mouth went dry and she did not know whether she should look at them or down in respect. She chose down but kept flicking her gaze up, looking for any clues as to what she should do.

She recognised Lord Jakalain. He was pale and dark circles ringed his eyes; he must have been up all night since the alarm. The second man was a patterner, from his robes, while the third was Swordmaster Erang, the chief armsman of the castle.

It was said the patterns of magic could not force a person to perform any act against their will. Did that mean they could not tell whether someone told the truth or not? She did not know. She simply prayed to the Mother that she would not be asked a question where she had to lie in response.

They took their places. The patterner flicked through the papers in front of him and took up the stylus. She stared in fascination as he fiddled with the end of it then found a small pot. He opened it and dipped the stylus in.

She glanced at the other men. Even the Lord Jakalain was watching the patterner, though whether he was impatient or simply waiting for him to be ready was impossible to tell. The swordmaster was watching her and she immediately cast her gaze back to the foot of the table where she could see them but not be looking at them.

"Sit down, Kantees," said Erang.

She hesitated. "I am sorry, Swordmaster, but I have been in the eyrie all morning and I do not wish to soil the chair. I beg your pardon."

"Kantees, is it?" said Lord Jakalain.

She trembled, never having been addressed directly by the lord before. "Yes, my lord."

"Sheesha's keeper."

"Yes, sire."

"Sit down, Kantees," he said. And where she might question the swordmaster, she dared not go against the lord himself. She shuffled to the front of the chair and gingerly placed her behind on it. She clasped her hands on her lap so that the men would not see them shake.

"What do you know of what happened last night, Kantees?" said Erang.

Kantees glanced at the patterner. He was not looking at her but was writing. It made her feel a little better, that he might only be there to keep a record of what happened here, not to perform any magic to divine the truth of her words.

"Kantees?"

"I know very little, sire. I heard the gossip in the kitchen. That is all."

"Really?"

She stared directly at the swordmaster. "I can tell you what I heard."

"That won't be necessary," said Lord Jakalain. "We have heard kitchen gossip a dozen times today."

She dropped her gaze to the floor again. "Yes, my lord."

"More than one person said they saw a *zirichak* flying in the night."

It seemed as if her heart stopped and she felt as if her very blood froze within her.

"I saw—" she almost hesitated as her tongue tripped on the lie, "—nothing, sire. I was asleep."

"You were not awakened by the alarm bell?" said Lord Jakalain.

"Sheesha was disturbed by the noise, sire, and upset. I did not go to see but tended to him."

Lies piled on lies. It was as if she were falling into a deep dark hole. But unless someone could claim they had seen Sheesha himself and recognised her on his back, there would be no more lies. She must keep it simple.

But Lord Jakalain was not finished. "You did not see the *tekrak*?"

"I heard stories in the kitchen, sire, but I did not believe them. How could there be a *tekrak* of such size?"

"I saw it with my own eyes, Kantees." He was angry. Lord Jakalain was angry with her.

She threw herself off the chair and prostrated herself on the rugs. "Sire, I am sorry. Beat me for my foolish tongue."

There was a long pause. She heard a chair scrape back on the stone floor and boots walking first away and then growing closer until they went quiet on the rugs. She could sense the man standing above her and she tensed herself for the first blow. She jumped as he caught hold of her shoulder.

"Get up, Kantees," said the Lord Jakalain. His voice was no longer angry, just tired.

She could not make her muscles obey her. His grip tightened and he pulled. She came up on to her knees but she kept her head down.

"I told you to get up." This time there was the iron command in his voice, as if she were testing his patience. She stood but kept her eyes down. Even so, she could see he had withdrawn a short distance.

"Many people saw the monstrous creature, Kantees, but there are many that did not and some remain as sceptical as you."

"I believe you, sire."

A short laugh from the swordmaster told her how inappropriate her comment was. That she, a mere slave, should give her approval to the words of her master. What her master said must be the truth.

Lord Jakalain returned to his seat and murmured something to the patterner who nodded. She wondered what they might be saying. Was it possible she was wrong, and that the patterner was able to tell truth from lies? But still they did not accuse her. And what in truth had she done wrong?

Apart from fly.

She had saved the castle, although she had not been quick enough to keep the lordling from being stolen away. She thought about how she had flown so far away from the castle; if she had spent less time enjoying the sensation perhaps Jelamie would still be with his family. If she had not wasted time with the raider on the tower, things might have been different.

"I am sorry," she said before she could stop herself.

"What do you mean?" said the swordmaster.

"I am sorry I cannot help, sire."

Swordmaster Erang shook his head, once more grimly amused by her presumption, but Lord Jakalain looked at her.

"Thank you, Kantees," he said. "And if you learn anything about the *zirichak* people claimed to see, you will speak to the swordmaster."

"Yes, sire," she said.

The men stood and filed out. The patterner took the papers with him. She must have been the last. They wouldn't talk to Gally because he was a simpleton, so she should be safe. Though it bothered her that Jelamie was taken.

She almost called them back. She almost admitted the truth because she knew a name: the Dunor. That was what the raider had said: *Are you with the Dunor?*

But she had no idea who the Dunor were. Was it a title? Just one person? A race? She had been to many competitions and she had never come across the name.

How could she not tell Lord Jakalain the truth?

But she couldn't. She had ridden Sheesha and the penalty was death. She did not want to die, but neither did she want the boy to suffer, no matter how unpleasant he was.

But another thought ran through her mind, a rebellious thought. She was a slave. The Taymalin had come all those years ago and invaded her people's island. They had become the masters and the Kadralin the enslaved. Why should she help them? What was the value of that stolen life against hers? Why was it more important?

She knew the answer.

It was because she had a choice. There were many things in her life over which she had no control; that was what being a slave meant.

And even though her position as a keeper meant an easier life than most, it could be cut short in a moment.

And it would be, if they discovered what she had done.

Never mind she had saved others from death. She had dared to do what only a Taymalin was permitted.

It was a different armsman that came to escort her back.

He stared at her strangely and insisted on checking her to ensure she had not stolen anything. She did not complain as the man touched her. It was not that he had the right; it was that she had no right to object.

She was the slave. He was one of the masters.

So why should she even consider helping the child of Lord and Lady Jakalain when she herself was nothing more than a possession? Something that could be bought and sold, or discarded when they no longer required her?

No, she thought as she suffered the indignities of a search that went on too long and investigated every part of her. *Since I am nothing but an object to them, there is nothing I can give them.*

5

Over the next few days she tried to ignore what had happened. It wasn't too hard. Since she spent most of her time in Sheesha's eyrie, and the next race had been postponed, she saw no one except those in the tower. There was nothing she needed to do beyond feed and clean the *zirichak*.

Sometimes, though, she would look out across the castle. Things had returned to normal on the surface and they had given up looking for Jelamie in the castle. He had not drowned in the well: they had checked. There was now little doubt he had been taken. Speculation as to why roamed from ransom—though no ransom had been demanded—to being used in some terrible ritual.

This was something Kantees also wondered. It seemed to her that it made no sense. Had the entire raid been mounted to capture a child of limited political value? But if that was the case, why send so many soldiers?

Of course no one else knew what she knew. They had not seen the thirty or more armsmen that had retreated to the *tekrak*.

Information about the monstrous flying plant was now common knowledge, though there were some among the staff who continued to disbelieve it. Romain being one of them, Kantees had to bite her tongue. She could not admit to having seen it.

"Gally saw it," said Galiko at breakfast on the third day after the raid.

"Gally is stupid and doesn't know what he's saying," said Romain unpleasantly. He was once more waiting for Gally to finish breakfast but this morning the youth seemed to be eating even slower than usual.

"Gally saw it," he repeated. "Big as a wall, all fire and smoking and soldiers."

At that moment Daybian walked into the kitchen, flanked by an 'honour guard'.

The sudden addition of guards for all the nobility was not fooling anyone. The Jakalain were scared, and the lord had insisted armsmen accompany every member of his family at all times.

The kitchen went silent in a wave as people realised he was there or noticed others had stopped talking and turned to see who had come in. Not that Daybian was an uncommon sight in the Ziri Tower.

"What's Gally saying?" he said to Romain, and Kantees tensed.

"Nothing, sire, just rambling like the fool he is."

Kantees panicked quietly. If they questioned Gally he was bound to let something slip. She hoped Daybian would find Romain's explanation convincing.

Galiko, like everyone else, had stood as the lordling entered and was looking at the ground, but unfortunately he wanted to defend himself against Romain's accusations.

"Gally saw the fire plant," said the boy.

"Don't listen, young master, you know he's a halfwit. Shut up, Gally."

"Honestly, I don't have time for this." Daybian sounded petulant and irritable as ever. Kantees wondered if he considered his baby brother to be a threat, but with ten years between them she could not see how even he could think it.

"Kantees?"

"Sire?"

"Is Sheesha ready to fly?"

"Keen to, sire, he has been shut up too long."

"Let's get to it then."

So she left her breakfast, barely touched, and hurried up the tower ahead of Daybian's more leisurely pace, though even he had to use the ladder to get into the eyrie. Sometimes Kantees wondered about that. If the castle eyries—most still unoccupied—had been designed for lords to fly their *zirichasa*, why did they not have separate ways in? In the castle there were special passages for the servants so the lords and ladies did not encounter slaves as they moved around.

But not in this tower. Not only that but the Ziri Tower was not made from the same stone as the rest of the castle, as if it didn't belong.

Whatever the reason, she knew she would reach the eyrie with plenty of time to spare to get Sheesha ready.

The *ziri* sensed her excitement as she clambered up and selected the riding tack. Sheesha crouched quietly as Kantees placed the saddle and buckled the straps. She settled the bridle over his muzzle and neck, and brought the reins back to the saddle.

The sound of boots on the ladders announced the arrival of Daybian and his men.

Sheesha shuffled nervously. Kantees saw he was arching his neck and rolling his eyes at the lordling and his men.

"Sire! Your men are unsettling Sheesha."

She moved up to Sheesha's neck and stroked his feathers, breathing gentle and soothing sounds, trying to calm him.

At least when it came to the *zirichak* Daybian was not a fool. He would not be such a good rider if he did not have empathy with his steed. However, the men were not that bright and, though he was the son of the lord, they argued with him. They did not want to go back down and disobey their master.

"Well, you cannot come out with me when I ride. And this eyrie has no other exits but that door into the air."

"But, sire…"

"One of you go up a floor, the other go down. You can guard me just as well like that."

One of them looked across at Kantees. "But what of the slave, sire?"

Daybian's anger at the comment was palpable though he barely raised his voice. "If Kantees wanted to cause me harm, she could have done it a hundred times before now. Now get out before I take the flat of my sword to you."

Finally they gave in. It was easier to give in to the Jakalain present than blindly follow the orders of the Jakalain who was not here. They were not slaves, of course. No one would willingly put a weapon in the hands of the subdued race; they were just paid armsmen.

"Ridiculous," muttered Daybian as he unbuckled his swordbelt and laid it on a hay bale. He stripped off the rest of the finery, then plucked the flying suit from the wall: the leather trousers and jacket that sealed his skin from the wind, and the helmet and special eye protections that he used when he was flying in a race.

Sheesha had settled once the armsmen left. He made a low rumbling sound deep in his throat as Daybian approached, but whether it was because he was pleased to see his master or excited about the prospect of flying after so many days of inactivity, there was no way of knowing. Kantees handed the reins to Daybian with a slight bow and went to undo the chain.

She heard Daybian speaking quietly to Sheesha, making sure he knew who was going to ride him. Sheesha rumbled again. There was no reason that Sheesha should not like Daybian, but the reaction always caused a little twinge of jealousy in Kantees' chest. But, she reminded herself, Sheesha had let her sleep with him.

She undid the chain and ran it through the first and second loops.

"Perhaps you are trying to kill me after all," said Daybian.

Kantees went cold. She looked up to where Daybian sat, poised in the saddle on Sheesha's back. His knees too high, it looked as if he were perching on a table. Kantees swallowed hard, realising she had forgotten to lengthen the stirrups after her ride.

She dropped the chain and rushed over, desperately trying to come up with an excuse that would sound reasonable. In a voice that almost squeaked with her panic, she blurted out her lie. "I am so sorry, my lord, I cleaned the tack and moved the buckles to remove the marks lower down."

Daybian laughed. "Don't worry, Kantees, these things happen."

How casually you joke about such a thing, she thought. *You have never been beaten or lashed.*

And then she cursed herself for being such a fool. The new falsehood was now added to all the others. She quickly lengthened the stirrups to their usual position, then went back to finish removing the chains. Finally, she unhooked them from the loop on Sheesha's leg.

She backed away as Daybian prepared to launch them from the eyrie. Sheesha screeched in delight. Daybian gave him his head and the *zirichak* ran at the eyrie door and leapt from it, his wings snapping open. He dropped for a moment and then powerful strokes lifted him back into sight.

Moments later he slid off to the left and disappeared from view, though another screech from him echoed across the castle.

6

"Have you heard?" said Libbibet as she doled out the breakfast porridge. Her face was drawn in concern.

"Heard what?"

"About Gally?"

Kantees drew in a breath. "What about Gally?"

"The armsmen took him this morning."

"What are you talking about?"

The porridge hung suspended from the spoon like a threat.

"They say he was working with the raiders."

"What?" Kantees almost shouted. "That's ridiculous, he can barely put two words together that make sense."

"You can say that," said Libbibet. "But he knows things about the raid. They'll get the truth out of him."

The porridge slopped into Kantees' bowl but she just put it down and turned, looking for Romain. He was sitting in his usual chair. She headed towards him as Libbibet chided her for forgetting her breakfast.

Kantees sat down in front of him.

"Heard then, have you?" He glanced up at her from his bowl. "To think we had a traitor right here with us."

"Gally's no traitor."

"Lord Jakalain says he is."

And that, for Romain, was that.

"What have they done with him?"

"Locked in the cells, I shouldn't wonder. They'll get what they can from him and hang him."

"How can you sit there and say that? Gally is our friend, he's one of us. He's Kadralin like you and me."

"Sssssh," muttered Romain. "You want to join him? I don't. And now I have to take one of those new keepers from the yearlings to help tend the old ones. Gally was stupid but he didn't complain."

"He wasn't stupid, he was just simple. He *is* just simple."

Kantees stood up. Indecision pulled at her. She needed to find out what was happening with Gally. Perhaps the rumours were wrong. Perhaps there was another reason he had been arrested. Sheesha needed her—but not straight away, since she had already done most of what was needed for the morning and she was not expecting Daybian today.

She looked back at Romain and sat again. "What's Dunor?"

He looked up at her with a frown. "What's what?"

"What's Dunor? Have you heard of it?"

"Dunor?" She nodded but he shook his head. "Never heard of it."

"Are you sure?"

"What's this about?" he asked suspiciously.

She ignored him and got to her feet again. Instead of heading back up the tower, she strode across the kitchen towards the door that led outside and to the main part of the castle. As she walked, she felt Romain's and Libbibet's eyes on her back.

She stepped through into the main courtyard. The day was bright with only a few broken clouds moving steadily across the sky.

What was she doing? She had no idea. She knew she wanted to see Gally but no idea how she could achieve it. There was no reason for them to let her see him. So she stood a few paces into the court-yard filled with people bustling about. All the activities of the castle were going on around her and she was not a part of any of them.

Considering Romain's reaction, she did not think she could even stop anyone to ask where to go. If they knew anything about Gally, they would already have made up their minds as to his guilt.

If Gally was hanged it would be her fault.

"Kantees."

She bowed her head automatically at the sound of Daybian's voice.

"Sire."

"What are you doing here?"

"I'm sorry, sire, I heard about Gally—Galiko."

"Yes, he is being questioned."

"I don't understand. He's just a halfwit. What could he possibly know? More likely he just dreamed something and believes it to be true."

"One would hope your loyalty to your master is as strong as that to your friend."

Loyal to my friend? Yes, I am that. But loyal to my owner? she thought. *I am as loyal as a knife. Romain might be happy with his lot, but I know that I am a slave and that does not please me.*

"As you say, sire."

"You wish to see him?"

"That was my intention, sire, but now that I am here I realise my foolishness. I was about to return to my place in the eyrie."

"Come with me." He strode off to the right to where a number of armsmen were lounging around a barrel.

Unable to argue, Kantees trailed in his footsteps.

The armsmen snapped to attention as Daybian approached. "Where is the slave Galiko being held? One of you can take me."

The most senior, a sergeant, by his armband, bowed. "Aye, my lord. This way."

Kantees did not fail to notice how fast things could be made to happen when one was the son of the lord and carried his authority. But it would be a long time before Daybian was in charge. His father was still quite young and strong.

The sergeant brought them to an entrance in the wall and then down into a tight corridor. As far as Kantees knew, the castle of the Jakalain had never been breached by enemies, certainly not within living memory, but the castle itself was designed for warfare. These narrow passages forced people to fight one at a time.

The walls were etched with patterns said to come alive if an enemy dared to enter. Quite what would happen, no one knew. Kantees doubted anything would; after so much time, the magic would be gone.

She gasped as they entered a room lit by torches and filled with devices to pierce, puncture, squeeze, and rend. It was not that she recognised any of the tools, but she knew what they were for by reputation. A torture chamber. The memories of the Kadralin slaves did not fade, and during the long winter nights they passed around stories about masters who took pleasure in the pain of their possessions. And then they would drink to the continuing health of the Jakalain, who did not do such things.

Unless they want to extract information from a halfwit who has none, she thought. Not true, though. Gally did have information and if he told them, for whatever reason, it would incriminate her. So why was she here, really? Was it for Gally, or for herself?

Both, probably. Gally would be scared. He couldn't possibly understand what was going on.

They passed through the torture room to a series of cells constructed with iron bars. There were a few ragged men and women here, and she had no idea who they were, except that they were Kadralin by their skin. They were all underfed, with their joints stark against their drawn skin, and listless. If they looked up at her at all it was with eyes that barely focused.

Then they reached Gally. He sat on the floor with his back to the other cells as if he did not want to see them. And well he might not. He had such a gentle spirit, the sight would hurt him.

"And here he is," said Daybian with a gesture of his hand as if he were conjuring her friend from a mist.

Unlike the ones who had been here longer, Gally turned at his voice, first taking in the lordling and then seeing her. His face lit up with hope, and her heart broke with the pain of it.

"Kantees." He always stretched the second part of her name almost as if he loved to say it. He reached through the bars and she took his hand.

"Are you all right, Gally?"

"No, Kantees, this is a bad place."

"I know."

Gally's eyes flicked to Daybian and back. "Gally told them," he said.

She felt a cold spear lance through her. But if he had told them about her, then she would not be on this side of the bars.

"What did you tell them?"

"Gally ride the *ziri*. Gally ring the bell."

Kantees closed her eyes and felt her heart pounding in her breast. Tears squeezed out between her lids. He was sacrificing himself for her. Sacrificing himself for her lies.

She looked at Daybian. As a slave she was forbidden to look him directly in the eye, but she did it anyway. "And you believe him? *Him?*"

Daybian shrugged. "It's nothing to do with me. He confessed to a crime and the punishment is death."

"But he's doesn't understand what he's saying. You can't trust what he says."

"As I say, it's none of my business."

"One day you will own this castle and the slaves in it. Would you rather be known as a tyrant who does not care?"

"You speak out of place."

She turned away and dropped her gaze to the floor. "I deserve to be beaten."

"Yes. You do," he said. There was a long pause. "I will mention the concern to my father but I doubt it will make any difference. A *zirichak* was seen and it is believed the rider rang the alarm bell. If it did not come with the raiders, it must have come from here. If Gally did not do it himself, he knows who did. Either way he is committing a crime."

Kantees held her tongue and hated herself for doing it. She wanted to say: *But why would he even admit it unless he was protecting some-one?* And the number of people that he could possibly be protecting was limited to only two: Romain and her.

"Is there anything I can do to make it better here?" she said. If she could not save Gally, perhaps she could at least reduce his suffering.

"There are no rules preventing you from bringing items for him."

"I am a slave, sire, I own nothing. He owns nothing."

"Food is allowed."

She nodded and squeezed Gally's hand. "I'll come back."

"No, Kantees. This is a bad place."

She gave him a smile. "It is a very bad place, Gally, so a visit from a friend is a good thing."

He pulled back his hand and returned to where he had been, with his back to everything.

She wanted to cry again but held it back. The dark eyes of the man in the cell next to Gally caught hers, and he stared at her. She hesitated as Daybian moved past her, and then followed him.

They came out into the daylight. Kantees thought it was strange. After being in the dungeon, she felt it should be night out here as well. And yet the morning was not even halfway gone.

"It is the spring feast tomorrow," said Daybian. "And the patterners say the Mother will feed the earth with her power. Very auspicious. They say."

"It is a Kadralin feast, sire."

"The power of the Mother cannot be denied," he said, "when her milk can be seen to come from … the moons."

She knew he had been going to use a more common term. The power of the Mother descended to the earth when Colimar and Lostimal stood together in the sky. It did not take a great deal of imagination to see them as a woman's breast. That's why the Kadralin called it the Mother's milk.

The ley-circle nearest to the castle was powerful and capable of twisting the nature of the world when the conjunction happened. It was only because Jakalain was in the middle of nowhere that it did not command more importance in the world.

Jakalain had little value to the Taymalin who occupied the Isle of Esternes.

"I had thought to take part in the festivities," he said.

The orgy, she translated. It was true the Kadralin could become quite wild during festivals, and it was common enough for the Taymalin to join in. She could see where this was going, and yet she could not directly refuse even though she had no desire to lie with him. She had no desire to lie with anybody. But when all was said, she was a slave and he was the son of her owner.

"I am sorry, but I cannot attend the feast. I will be tending to Sheesha," she said. "He does not like to be disturbed at night, and it makes him irritable the next day. The noise upsets him."

"I will come up to the eyrie. We will watch the feeding of the earth from there. It would provide an excellent view."

And now I have made it worse, she thought. *He will expect me to be there.*

"As you wish, sire," she said. She would just have to hope that he would get caught up with someone else or decide it was not worth the effort. She shook her head as she walked away. He was a man. The opportunity to lie with a woman, and one that he had just convinced himself desired it, would be the strongest attraction.

She had condemned herself.

7

*L*ater that day Kantees scrounged some food from Libbibet and went off to the cells.

Since she was not accompanied by Daybian, she was stopped by the guards. She wished they could be given a lashing for the things they said to her. But she could not respond, or she would have been on the receiving end of the lash—something she had thus far managed to avoid in her life.

However, it was when one of them suggested she might be "available" for the spring festival that she simply suggested he would need to ask Lord Daybian for her use after he had finished with her. That shut him, and the rest of them, up. And she continued with no further molestation.

At least that wasn't a lie, she thought, although if she could think of a way out of Daybian's plan for her, she would take it.

There was a solution, she knew. She could tell the truth. If she revealed that it was she who had ridden Sheesha and saved the castle, then Gally would be safe and she might be able to hope that she would get away with a severe lashing—since the fact she had saved the castle might count in her favour. She sighed. It was hopeless, either Gally died, or she did.

And Jelamie would still be lost.

So instead she could confess to Daybian when he arrived and then throw herself off the tower. That would solve all the problems —except Jelamie, again, but that really wasn't her fault since she had not caused him to be kidnapped. That was someone else's problem.

She came down into the cell and found Gally still facing the corner.

"Gally?" she said. He turned and his face lit up at the sight of her. He climbed to his feet and came to the bars. She passed the packages through.

"It's just some food," she said. "Libbibet said I could bring it for you."

"Thank you, Kantees."

The man in the cell next door was looking at her again. It wasn't that she knew every slave and servant in the castle by sight but she was sure he wasn't one of them. The cut of his clothes was unusual and even his face seemed out of place. His skin was very dark even for a Kadralin—it was like midnight.

She turned her attention back to Galiko. "Have they hurt you?"

He shook his head and focused on the shrivelled apple which was one of the few remaining from last season. The kitchen staff kept the apples on trays in the cellars. They dried up but stayed edible, though mostly they were put into pies. It was still a long time before there would be any fresh.

There was bread, too, and a stone bottle of water.

She moved along the iron bars to get away from the one who watched her, but there really wasn't enough space in Gally's cell.

"What have you told them?"

"Gally kept your secret, Kantees. Gally won't let them kill you."

Once more she felt like crying. "You should have just said you didn't know anything."

He looked at her as if she were talking nonsense. "Master Daybian knew. They said they would hurt me if Gally did not say."

"Daybian was there?"

"Master Daybian came with armsmen."

"Bastard," she muttered. He must have caught the end of the conversation in the kitchen—heard more than he claimed to have.

"But I did not tell the secret, Kantees." He was almost pleading with her to approve of what he had done.

She sighed and smiled. She reached through the bars and put her hand on his shoulder. "You did a very brave thing, Gally."

"Like a hero."

Her smile grew wider. "Yes, like a real hero."

And that settled it. It was impossible to let him suffer for what she had done. Her lies had got them into this mess, so she was going to have to think of a way out of it.

But the only thing she could think of was to run away.

She glanced at the man in the cell next door. He was still staring and her frustration overflowed in a verbal attack. "Why are you staring at me?"

He did not flinch. Not even a blink. Instead, he climbed to his feet. "Greetings to the Lady Kantees." And then he bowed with one hand on his stomach and the other giving a broad gesture. She had never seen anything like it— not directed towards herself, at least. There had been some lord at a race last year who had not had any *zirichasa* to race, but he had bet heavily. His mannerisms had been like this, bold and flowery.

"I think you're mistaking me for someone else, or having a jest," she said. "Now if you don't mind I would appreciate it if you stopped staring at me and left me with my friend."

"As you wish."

He turned his back on her and stepped to the far side of his cell. Kantees was taken aback. She was ready for an argument but he had pulled the wind from her wings.

After a moment she turned back to Gally who had finished the food and was washing it down with the water. She wanted to ask him what the other fellow was in for but she didn't think Gally could cope with the question. His viewpoint was always focused on himself.

"I'll bring some more tomorrow," she said. She hated to go but she had her own duties and she couldn't leave Sheesha for long. "Look, Gally, if they ask you again, why don't you say you've forgotten and that you made it all up."

"Gally must protect you, Kantees. They mustn't hurt you."

"But—" she started, then realised it was pointless. He was so single-minded, once he started on a course it was almost impossible to get him to change. Unless, of course, you could distract him so thoroughly he forgot what he was doing. If they kept on asking him, there was little chance of him forgetting.

She had barely gone five paces when the other man stopped her.

"Kantees."

"Dropped the 'lady' already?"

"I can use it, if you wish."

"I don't."

"I am here to offer my help," he said. "My master sent me because he knew you would be in need."

She turned on him with her hands on her hips. "I don't know what game you're playing, but I can't help you get out of here. In case you hadn't noticed the colour of my skin, I'm just as much a slave here as you. There's no point trying. I can't help you."

"I do not think you were listening."

"I heard every word you said but you seem to have failed to see that you are the one that is in a cell. I am on the outside."

"Yet you are more trapped than I," he said.

Kantees could not think of anything to say so she stood silent, her jaw twitching, until she blurted at him, "I really do not have time for this."

And left.

She hurried across the courtyard, ignoring the jeers of the armsmen. Once through the kitchen she climbed the ladders to the eyrie. Sheesha had messed twice and she spent the time clearing it up, trying to understand what was happening.

Once the shovelling and sweeping was complete she fetched the powder that was intended to reduce the number of parasites on Sheesha's body. She was not sure whether it worked since Sheesha's skin seemed to be home to a constant supply of the horrible little bugs.

Some of which were not so little.

It was an unending task and possibly the one she enjoyed least. It usually ended with her exploring the base of the feathers, trying to squash (preferably) or grab (if necessary) the little things to remove them. Romain had explained that in the wild the *zirichasa* would preen one another, just like smaller birds did, in order to remove the parasites. For creatures in captivity, the keepers had to do it.

And when she was finished, she had to put up with Sheesha attempting to return the favour, prodding every part of her body, trying to get to her skin around the clothes—perhaps he thought clothes were feathers—and then nipping at her, which was occasionally painful but she was sure he didn't mean to hurt her. Once or twice he had nipped hard enough to elicit blood and a cry of pain. When that happened he would rub his muzzle against her as if apologising.

As she systematically worked her way up his spine between his wings, she realised how much she cared for the beast. And then she felt sad. The only solution she could think of was to run away, leaving a message behind saying that Gally was innocent and only trying to protect her in his childlike way.

Running away meant she would have to leave Sheesha—and she couldn't think of any other apprentice that was ready to look after him.

There were so many problems with that plan—it wasn't even a plan, it was just an idea. In the first place she would have trouble getting out of the castle. Her job was to look after Sheesha. The only time she went out was when there were races.

And there was no way she could leave a message without telling someone because she couldn't write. And there was no one she could trust except Gally, and he would not be able to cope, even assuming they accepted what he said, which wasn't going to happen since he was already under suspicion.

Finally, she had nowhere to go and no way to get there. If she did manage to get out of the castle, a runaway slave would be hunted down in no time at all. There was always one or two every year who decided they would make a run for it. But the Jakalain land was nowhere, and apart from the orchards there weren't even forests to hide in within a tow or three days of travel. She didn't *think* there was. But who would know? People either followed the road, or travelled by patterner's path. And she had never used the roads.

She sighed and lay down along the length of Sheesha's back,

letting the warmth from his feathers flow into her. She yawned. The worry of the last few days had meant she was not sleeping very well.

Sheesha moved and lay down too, with her on his back. He let out a gentle grumble that vibrated through her. It made her feel relaxed.

Of course, if she escaped on Sheesha's back she could get away easily and no one would be able to catch her.

She blinked her eyes open and stared at the feathers in front of her face. It was true, she could do that. But that would mean leaving Gally. And then she thought of the crazy man in the cell. What if he wasn't crazy? What if he could help?

No, of course not. He was in a cell. There was nothing he could do.

You are more trapped than I.

His words haunted her. He did not act like someone who was trapped. He seemed totally at ease. And his clothes, in spite of their odd appearance, were of the highest quality. Why was he even locked up?

He was a slave, he had admitted as much himself with the mention of his own master. Yet he did not act like a slave.

8

Kantees looked back up the passageway towards the torture room. This was the third day she had come to this place and it had gained a strange familiarity. All the years she had lived in the castle she had hardly ever set foot inside the main defensive walls. Now she was accustomed to it. The guards recognised her and no longer checked her—though that might have been because of her comment about Daybian.

She was carrying food for Gally again. She did not understand why they kept him locked up. Romain was struggling to keep abreast of the daily chores, and he had even insisted she help him.

Moving hay bales was hard work but she had been doing it since she was young and she was easily as strong as Romain himself. Perhaps that was not saying a great deal, he was getting old. Certainly she was stronger than most of the apprentices.

And the four older *zirichasa*—Romain's charges—liked her. It was not that they were particularly old, but they could no longer race. They seemed to appreciate her attention when she spoke to them and scratched their necks. Daybian had had his father buy them as breeding stock. The male and one of the females—Looesa and Shingul—had been winners in a few races, though not sufficient to make them very expensive.

The apprentices tended the yearlings that were their offspring. Sheesha was not related to any of them as far as she knew.

Romain insisted the apprentices were too incompetent to help and that she must do it. So she spent some time before the midday meal working with him. There was not much to be done. She guessed that Romain probably did none of it when he had Gally to help—and that he chose Gally over any of the others because the simple lad would not question Romain's laziness.

So she was later than she intended.

And Galiko was looking for her through the bars as she came down. Her glance backward confirmed there were no armsmen watching or listening. She was not entirely sure how she felt about the other prisoners. They were criminals of one sort or another. Mostly slaves who had been caught pilfering. Though they might have been wrongfully accused—that was very common.

If they thought she was up to something, they might think it would ease their punishment if they traded the information. But the Taymalin were strict, so she doubted negotiation was acceptable. The slightest hint that any of them knew anything of interest would lead to torture.

However, she did not want to take the chance.

She greeted Gally and gave him the food. Then she leaned against the cage with her back to the other man—she did not even know his name.

"What help can you offer?" she said in a low voice she hoped would not carry.

"You have reconsidered."

"Something needs to be done."

"And you are the one to do it?"

"Stop playing games and answer my question."

"Have you thought of a way out of the castle?"

"Yes, but I cannot leave my friend to the benevolence of my master."

"No, indeed," he said. "The Taymalin are well known for their fatal kindness."

"What's your name?"

"Yenteel."

"Why are you here?"

"My master is interested in you."

"I don't know your master."

"No, but he knows you."

"How is it possible that he knows me?"

"I expect he saw you at the races."

"If your master is that interested, he could just offer Jakalain a price for me."

"Sadly he is not that rich."

"And how did you end up in here?"

"It is difficult to get an invitation into the castle when you are a slave alone."

"That doesn't answer my question."

"Oh, you want the precise details? I propositioned one of the armsmen—a captain."

She blinked. Surely he did not mean what he had just said. She turned and looked at him. "You *propositioned?*"

"I suggested he might like to join me for the night."

Kantees could think of nothing to say.

"The fellow seemed to think I had insulted him and so did not take me up on it, but he did put me where I wanted to be. They considered it a great joke that I would indeed be spending the night at his home. I considered it a great joke as well, that their behaviour was so predictable."

She grinned. "What if he had accepted your offer instead?"

Yenteel shrugged. "I did choose the most handsome one."

"Oh." She shook the mental image loose. "How could being in here be of any help? You did not know I would be coming down here. I did not even know myself."

"It was in the pattern."

Then she really did laugh. "You expect me to believe you can read the world's pattern?"

"You are not required to believe anything if you do not wish to," he said. "Besides, I did not say that I could read it. I only have to know someone who does."

"If I knew the world's pattern I would not squander that knowledge in getting myself put into a prison cell," she said. "Anyway, did the pattern say anything about how you were going to get out?"

"Of course," he said. "You."

Gally had finished eating and just sat watching the two of them talk. She wondered if he was able to follow what was being said. Probably not; that's why he didn't interrupt. He couldn't be part of it. She was not sure even she wanted to be a part of it. The last thing she wanted was to think her actions were being manipulated by someone else.

"Let's say I could get you and Gally out of the castle," she said. "Can you get out of the cell?"

"Yes."

"How?"

"That's for me to know when the time comes."

"Fine, have it your own way," she said. "Can you be ready tomorrow evening?"

"During the feeding, yes."

"After," she said. "I am meeting someone."

It hadn't been a decision as much as a feeling that had been growing on her. The pressure of the missing boy, that Gally was simply being held and neither released nor punished. A feeling had come over her like a day when the clouds were low and it was as if the whole sky pressed down.

The feeding tomorrow would be the best time. The magic would be so wild and dangerous that the patterners wouldn't be able to do anything.

"Kantees?"

She was shocked from her reverie as Daybian came down the corridor. Why on earth was he here? Was he following her, keeping track of her? He was so relaxed, so sure of himself. Arrogant.

Did he know she had been talking to Yenteel? But the prisoner was already on the other side of his cell, looking at the floor, drawing no attention to himself.

And then Daybian grinned at her. "Tomorrow night."

She growled inwardly. He was still planning to take her and no doubt use the excuse of the "wild" Kadralin if there were any consequences. The blame could easily be shifted to those with no responsibility or no choice in the matter.

"When?"

"Unfortunately for us, I must attend the feast and witness the feeding proper with my family. Then I shall come to you."

"What is being done about finding your brother?" she asked and was taken by the genuine heaviness that seemed to come over him.

He shook his head. "It is difficult to know what can be done. The raiders are long gone, and there was nothing to identify the ones that were slain—save that they were Taymalin."

For which we can be grateful, thought Kantees. *If the attackers had been Kadralin every one of us would be suspect and liable for torture.*

"I am sorry," she said even though it was not the place for a slave to feel sympathy for a master. They might not rebel, but they might cheer inside when a master suffered. It detracted from their own pain. But it was true, she was sorry.

Daybian put his hand on her shoulder—almost as one would with a companion, a friend—and gave a gentle squeeze. "No one knows where to look. And there has been no ransom demand."

He dropped his hand and the lascivious grin returned. "Until tomorrow, Kantees."

With that he strode away. Kantees stared after him.

"He will upset your plans," said Yenteel behind her.

"No, he won't."

"You may have to kill him."

She turned and took hold of the bars. Yenteel was there, close, with his midnight skin and brown eyes, taller than she was.

"Whatever I do," she said, "it will not be because of anything you say I should or should not. I will not cause the Jakalain any more pain."

"You are a slave."

"And to act like a master makes me no better than them."

It seemed he had no response to that. He turned away and went to sit in the corner. And whether it was to contemplate on the world's pattern, or to nurse his failure, she really could not care.

She turned back to Gally and he asked her simple questions about the people in the tower and she answered them to the best of her ability. She truly did not take much notice of the gossip.

9

*I*n truth she had no reason to stay with Sheesha during the Mother's feeding. It had happened plenty of times before and Sheesha had never given any indication he was upset by the white lights from the sky.

It usually happened at night. Tonight it was overcast, but that did not seem to make any difference to the magic that drove it.

Nobody knew what the feeding was. Leastways, if the patterners did know they kept it a secret. And if the wisdom of the Kadralin had fathomed its mysteries, that knowledge must have been lost when they were enslaved. She hoped the latter was the truth. She would rather it was her people that knew and had forgotten, than the Taymalin's patterners.

She really knew nothing about her own people. She only knew slaves and slavery.

The sky had been dark for a long time. The opposite wall of the castle, where the *tekrak* had landed, was full of people—Taymalin— while the slaves able to do so would be watching from the windows.

Her vantage point was the best, except perhaps for Romain's above her.

The ley-circle was not visible even in daylight since it was behind a ridge, and the clouds were now thick and low.

No sound accompanied a feeding save for the excited screams, shouts, and cheers of the people who watched. She could feel the time approaching. It was a tension in the air. The patterners had already declared that this was going to be a powerful occurrence and everyone who lived close to the circle had been ordered to leave.

The power of a feeding warped the earth. She had never seen it but she was told there were the remains of a castle closer to the circle. What remained of its stone walls were twisted and melted. Strange plants grew nearby, too: abominations. Perhaps it had been stronger once.

Then the world went white.

A column of light came into existence, flooding the world with a brilliance that hurt the eyes. The castle was illuminated in a blaze of pure white, the shadows utter black.

As her eyes adjusted she could see the moving lines within the column as if it were composed of individual strands leading down from the heavens beyond the clouds. And up there, the light emanated from the shape formed by the two moons.

She heard the disjointed chant floating up from below: *"Mother Earth, feed me; Mother Earth, clothe me; as the milk of the Earth feeds her children in the sky, so feed me."*

She joined in and tonight she felt as if it were really true. As if she were being fed by the power of the Mother.

She closed her eyes and the brightness shone through them. She smiled.

And the light winked out.

Below and across the land the revelries began. For some it would become an orgy. For herself, she had to deal with Daybian, but it would take him a while to get here. So she had to be prepared.

And then she stopped. She could not truly believe she was planning to steal Sheesha and the others. But what choice did she have? If she was going to free Gally and Yenteel, even though she felt no real obligation to the latter, she could only do it with the *ziri*.

She hurried up the ladder, past her loft, to the old ones' eyrie. Romain was not here because he had gone off to the celebrations, just as she could have done if she had not had other plans, or been trying to avoid Daybian.

White light flickered momentarily through the gaps in the eyrie door. This happened as well. Sometimes the power was so great, the conjunction of the moons so perfect, that additional bursts of power —leftovers—still erupted from time to time as the moons moved slowly apart.

Looesa and Shingul seemed pleased to see her. They made no objection when she fetched their tack from the walls and slipped it onto them. She sighed. This was a terrible idea. She did not even know if she could get them to follow her to the ground without riders.

But it was the only idea she had. And she had to rely on Yenteel to get out of his cell, release Gally, and deal with any guards though hopefully they would be too busy and it wouldn't be necessary.

"Kantees!"

She jumped. Daybian was below. He was earlier than she expected and must have been in a hurry to see her. His loins must have goaded him. She sighed.

"I am tending to the old ones. I will be down in a moment."

"I'll come up."

"No, please, I'm nearly done. Talk to Sheesha."

She tightened the chest strap on Looesa who now kept nudging her, excited to be going out.

"You have to wait," said Kantees. "I'll be back and then we'll go."

She looked at Jintan, the third of the set. He was significantly older than the other two. He had come as part of the auction lot with them. She did not understand why, since he did not add any value. She shook her head and patted him on the neck, he was very good-natured. He croaked at her and butted her with his nose.

"Not today, Jintan," she said quietly. No one rode him anymore. He was allowed out on a tether only and seldom even then. *He must be losing his strength without the exercise.*

As she climbed down the ladder she heard Daybian murmuring to Sheesha. She smiled. At least he was good with *ziri*, but then Sheesha wouldn't have tolerated him if he wasn't. They were sensitive creatures.

Daybian was still dressed in his finest and rubbing Sheesha under his chin. His clothing was completely inappropriate for the eyrie. He would get filthy, but it would be up to someone else to clean his clothes so why should he care? Yet if the cleaner failed to remove every stain, they would be the one punished.

The smile she had for him over Sheesha dropped from her face. There was little light in here so he wouldn't see her angry frown. She still had to deal with him and quickly, since the staff on duty would soon return to their posts.

"Have you ever taken part in the revels following a feeding, Kantees?" he asked. She did not have to see his smug grin to know it was there. She could hear it in his voice.

"I watch the feeding from here," she said. "I have no reason to join in with the Taymalin."

"I think you Kadralin have more fun."

She took a deep breath. It was her position, as a slave, to be agreeable and obey her master's every command. But as Sheesha's keeper she had some authority. Her word was followed with regard to his care and development. And Daybian was someone she had to talk to as almost an equal since he was the rider. She knew he liked it when she argued with him, because being male he liked to fight for things—as long as he won.

"You are only interested because you wish for more exercise."

"It is only through exercise that I win races."

"But there is more to life than winning."

"Not for me."

"Always it comes back to you. Is no one else important?"

"You are important to me, Kantees."

"Only because I help you win races."

"But not the important ones, yet."

She sighed. She was tired of his games. "I do not want to be ridden, sire."

There. She had said it. She had denied her master.

She half expected him to be angry and to force himself on her. But she watched his shadow detach itself from Sheesha's and move towards her slowly.

"Do you not find me handsome?"

"I value my position, sire. What if I were to become with child? I could not look after Sheesha, so could not help you win your races."

"That is a clever excuse."

"Sire," she said. "You can do whatever you want with me and I will not resist. I am your slave."

The shadow turned away and his voice came to her more echoing than before. "I do not wish to force you."

No, he wanted her to go to him willingly, as if she wanted it. "There would be no force required, sire."

"But would you caress me in your passion?"

"I would not resist you."

"And that is the greatest insult of all."

Kantees picked up the shovel she used for shifting Sheesha's droppings. As she took a few steps towards Daybian, he heard her footsteps. She had the strongest feeling that he thought she had relented and was coming to give him the satisfaction he desired.

She swiped him across the head with the shovel and he went down with the slightest cry of pain.

She checked him and made sure there was no blood. She had hit him with the flat part; after all, she felt no malice towards him personally, and she could not afford for him to die. If that happened they really would come after her and keep hunting her until she too was dead.

He was not unconscious but the blow appeared to have knocked his wits from him. She tied him up with spare tack. He might have to spend the rest of the night here but they would find him in the morning when they came looking for her.

His gaze was reproachful as she tied one final thong around his head, holding a rag in position in his mouth. She did not want him alerting anyone too early.

"I'm sorry," she said as she tucked a saddle under his head so he was not too uncomfortable. "I didn't want to do this but you insisted on coming up here tonight."

He mumbled something through the gag.

"This has nothing to do with you," she said.

A short annoyed noise.

"If you weren't being dictated to by what's between your legs, you could still be down there having a nice time."

Something, something, something.

"Well, I didn't want to," she said. "And if you had any sensitivity at all you would have realised that."

Indignation.

"No, you're not."

As she was tightening the final straps, she turned to him.

"In a few years I might have wanted to, perhaps, Daybian." There was a grunt. "I will call you Daybian now, because it doesn't matter. I have broken so many rules already and there are more to come."

This time she was not going to ride unprepared. She collected a set of Daybian's riding gear and pulled it on over her clothes—there was plenty of space. Then she unearthed a bag containing a water bottle and tinderbox from where she had hidden it in the hay.

The time had come.

She went to release the chain that held Sheesha, then squatted down in front of Daybian. His eyes flickered with reflected moonlight.

"I have to explain something so just listen and don't interrupt," she said. "I was the one who rang the alarm bell when the raiders came. Sheesha woke me and insisted I go with him. You can believe that or not, I don't care. Gally saw me and that's all, he's innocent. How could he be anything else?"

She sighed. "I want to put things right. I wasn't quick enough to save Jelamie from being taken, and for that I'm sorry. If I had admitted anything of what happened I would be killed for riding Sheesha. And Gally too perhaps, for not admitting the truth, yet he only did it to save me."

She stood up and went to Sheesha. She put her foot in the saddle and climbed up. After she had tightened the belt and gathered the reins, with Sheesha prancing back and forth ready to go, she turned to Daybian again.

"There is one thing. The raider on the bell tower said something to me before he died. I don't know what it meant but I'm going to find out, and I will rescue Jelamie if he is still alive."

In the dark she could not tell his expression, so she turned and gave Sheesha his head. The *ziri* launched himself from the eyrie.

10

The thrill of being on Sheesha's back again was wonderful. But she could not spend any time enjoying it. She wheeled him back to the tower, not caring if anyone saw her. He thought they were going back to his eyrie so she had to force him up to the one above.

The *zirichasa* often called to one another in the tower. Almost as if they were having a conversation. Since Sheesha was the strongest of the four he seemed to have precedence. Kantees did not know how the *ziri* arranged their flocks in the wild, particularly since the yearlings seemed to have no organisation whatsoever.

She dismounted and unchained Looesa, then Shingul. They did not try to leave, but she could only hope they would follow once she and Sheesha were in the air.

She lengthened their leads as far as she could and, still holding them, remounted Sheesha and buckled herself in.

"Come on, then," she said encouragingly as she nudged Sheesha towards the opening. The other two followed as she pulled on their reins, though once Sheesha jumped she would have to let go; otherwise her arm would probably be torn from its socket.

It was the moment of truth.

"Go!" she hissed at Sheesha and, "Come on!" to the others.

Sheesha dived out—she was getting used to that—and wheeled higher in a spiral, which she hadn't instructed him to do but seemed a good idea. On the first turn, Sheesha screeched and the sound echoed across the castle.

Kantees groaned. She had hoped she could start her rescue with no one noticing but there was no chance of that now. Everyone would be looking into the sky, although all they'd see was the great shadow of the dragon against the clouds.

Two more screeches as Looesa and Shingul burst from the eyrie with their leads trailing from their heads. They moved in unison with Looesa slightly in the lead, then wheeled into the spiral and followed Sheesha as he climbed.

Kantees muttered a satisfied, *"Good"*. At least that part of the plan was working as she had hoped. She wouldn't be happy until she was away from this place. And that thought made her falter as Sheesha continued to climb.

She was a runaway slave. She could be killed by anyone and no one would care. Many would be grateful. Even those of her own people would be grateful because she was causing trouble. By her actions she could bring down more trouble on their heads. The masters would be more cautious, their punishments would be harsher.

And it would be her fault.

It was too late to worry about it. She leaned forwards and pushed Sheesha out of his climb. She looked back and found the other two flanking them. They had flown beyond the walls. Below were armsmen on the ramparts, heads craned back staring at the three *ziri*, no more than dark shapes.

They dared not shoot because they did not know who was riding. It might be Daybian. Unfortunately that would change very soon. She leaned over Sheesha's neck and looked down as she brought him round in a circle. The figures below were like beetles crawling across a stone.

The tower allowed her to orient exactly where she was looking: the entrance to the cells.

She recognised Gally from his shuffling gait as he stepped out, with a taller and lankier figure beside him: Yenteel with a bag clutched in one hand. His bag? Perhaps Sheesha's cry had alerted the foreigner.

With a shifting of her weight and gentle words of encouragement she put Sheesha into a dive heading for the main tower and its entrance on the far side of the castle courtyard. The wind swept across her face but the helmet kept it under control and, with her gloves and leather clothing she barely felt the cold on her skin.

She allowed herself a quick glance back, and still Looesa and Shingul were with them. As far as Kantees could tell they were exactly the same distance from one another and from Sheesha's tail as they had been during the climb. She turned back as she felt Sheesha's muscles tensing up. She had not realised how fast they were going and the opposite wall was coming at them fast. Sheesha did not need encouragement in the turn.

The face of the guard at the hall entrance took on a look of horror as Sheesha whipped round in a blast of air which knocked him from his feet.

This was the most dangerous and stupid thing she had done in her entire life.

She reined Sheesha in. His head lifted, he backwinged hard, and they landed with a scrape of talons on stone directly in front of Yenteel and Gally. Behind her she heard the other two touch down together. Yenteel's long, loose hair was blown back and the supercilious grin he had worn in the cells was gone. The shock of the three *ziri* landing in front of him had seen to that.

Good.

She glanced around. Every face in the courtyard was directed towards them. Mouths gaped, some with fear, most with astonishment. Nobody was shouting yet, but she knew that would come.

Gally was backing away. She had expected that. "Gally, help Yenteel mount Shingul! Now!"

He jumped at her command and moved as she directed. Unfortunately, that meant the armsmen's eyes were now directed at Kantees instead of the *ziri*. They were coming to their feet, or standing straighter, hands moving to the swords at their sides.

"Hurry, Gally," she said as he went past. He had not yet queried the fact she was riding Sheesha, and getting someone else mounted was something he had done before, and therefore not outside the bounds of his experience. The next stage would be harder.

She had chosen the older mounts, instead two of the larger yearlings, for several reasons—not least because Gally worked with them so they knew him. She put Yenteel on Shingul because she was the more docile of the two and had sometimes been used to give rides to guests. Not that they ever flew her—either they knew what they were doing and did not need help, or they were given the ride just for the thrill. And sometimes the ride was given to a wife or a mistress to persuade their lords to give money as an investment on the promise of wins in future races.

The armsmen were looking at one another. Clearly they did not want to take on, and possibly damage, such a valuable animal. But they had recognised Kantees, and were moving forwards—slowly and carefully. Perhaps she could have managed with just one more *ziri* but saddles meant they could only carry one person each.

She pulled back on the reins and Sheesha went up on his hind legs, head high, and wings out. He beat them defiantly and screeched again. Here, inside the enclosing walls of the castle, the screech echoed, re-echoed, and redoubled. It was deafening.

The armsmen drew back, though she knew the noise would not stop them for long. Someone shouted. "Ropes! Nets!"

She looked back and saw Yenteel was in place. He did not look happy. Gally had gathered up the reins and put them in his hand, not that he had any clue what to do with them. This was a problem, but if Shingul did not take off with Sheesha, it wasn't her fault.

"Gally, ride Looesa!"

The old *ziri* looked up at the sound of his name, first at her, then at Gally who hesitated and stared at her. He knew he was not allowed to ride. He might not understand that it was a death sentence to do it, but he knew it was forbidden to him.

"Look, Gally, I'm riding. You can do it."

More shouting. A couple of men had emerged from the building carrying a net between them. From the other direction were armsmen on either side of someone swinging a noose with a skill that showed her he knew what he was about.

Not yet, she thought. "Gally! Quick! Get on Looesa!"

Then Looesa called to him, with the same grunting sound Sheesha had used the morning he had woken her during the raid. Gally looked at Looesa. The old *ziri* dropped his whole front body so it was along the ground, making it easy for the lad. The dragon grunted again.

"Looesa wants you to ride, Gally, you wouldn't say no to him, would you?"

The confusion in Gally's face cleared and he grinned. Moments later he was getting into the saddle, having gathered up the reins on his way.

There was a scream from the armsmen to the front and they ran forwards with their nets. Sheesha reared and bellowed again. This time Looesa and Shingul joined in and the courtyard echoed like the mountains with their cries.

"Gally ready!" he shouted sounding excited and happy.

Out of the corner of her eye Kantees caught a movement. The man with the noose had got within a dozen strides of her and the loop of rope was in the air. It flew true. Kantees was buckled into a saddle on the back of a huge creature. She could not dodge.

Sheesha's head whipped round and snapped on the rope. The loop dangled from his teeth. Swinging his head back the other way, the dragon ripped the rope from the man's hands, and a scream of pain from his throat. Staggering away, he pressed his palms under his arms.

Kantees gave Sheesha a kick. "Up!"

The powerful *ziri* went back on his hind legs and as his wings beat down, he leapt into the air. "Looesa! Shingul! Come!" she screamed at the top of her voice though it felt insignificant in the cold air. Yet still, she heard her words echo from the walls.

Each wingbeat forced Sheesha higher, slowly at first, then picking up speed. She allowed herself a glance behind and saw the older *ziri* climbing too, in perfect formation. She sighed with relief. They were going to make it.

They passed the top of the walls and she heard a whistling thrum. Then another. Arrows. They must have decided allowing slaves to escape was worse than damaging the *ziri*. Then a dozen more arrows whistled past. Yenteel cried out in pain.

The sound of arrows dropped away as they passed out of range. But they were still above the castle. They needed a direction, and she had one. It was not much of a choice but it was better than no choice at all.

She leaned forwards so that Sheesha was flying horizontally instead of upwards. Below them the castle looked so small she felt she could reach out and crush it in her fist. But she did not wish to do that. Not right now.

She got her bearings from the river below and set their course to follow where the giant *tekrak* had gone, even though it had left days before.

Once they were established and Sheesha needed no further guidance, she turned in the saddle to look at Gally. He was still grinning. Clearly the idea that the *ziri* had wanted him to ride was still a thing of pleasure to him. She envied him his simplicity.

Yenteel was not in a good way, however. It looked as though the arrow that had hit him had pinned his right arm to his chest. He was holding the reins in his other hand and he was conscious, but that's all she could tell in the dark.

With the blessing of the Mother, she thought, *I will make all this right. Though I have no idea how.*

11

Kantees was not sure how long they had travelled, but the clouds had turned into ragged fragments and the light of Colimar reflected dirty red on their underside as the moon sank below the horizon. The plains below them undulated in dark folds, and they crossed a dozen rivers. To their right were the mountains, looming and threatening as always. But in every other direction, the rolling hills with the occasional wooded area huddled in a valley.

And, once or twice, the light of dwellings. They had flown over a village where smoke drifted from the chimneys of the buildings.

She had no idea where they were or how far they had come but she could not let Yenteel suffer any longer. He moaned occasionally as the *ziri* were buffeted by winds, and besides, her legs were also stiff and sore. Much more of this and she would not be able to walk.

So she let Sheesha descend and choose one of the valleys. It would have wood for a fire, water from the stream, and be sheltered from the elements.

There were holes in her plan, and she was aware of them, but she had focused on getting them out of the castle since nothing else mattered if that could not be achieved. The next problem was food, not only for the riders but their mounts. She had no idea how she would feed them.

Back at the castle they were given the carcasses of animals that they ripped to shreds and gobbled down. Even the bones were consumed after being cracked in their powerful jaws. They were so strong they could easily escape once the group had landed and the riders dismounted.

But perhaps that did not matter. They could continue on foot.

The dark ground came up below them. Sheesha flapped his wings hard and landed with the lightest bump. Moments later there was a cry of pain from Yenteel as Shingul came down.

Unbuckling herself as quickly as possible she jumped down and collapsed into the soft grass as her legs failed to support her. It was damp here. Must have been raining.

Grabbing Sheesha's feathered wing for support she pushed herself to her feet and staggered across to Shingul. Yenteel's face looked ghostly in the dark as if even the colour of his skin had been drained away. The saddle harness was sticky with his blood, but his harsh breathing told her he was not dead.

"Gally, help me," she said. Even with Yenteel unbuckled she did not know how she would get him to the ground without aggravating his wound. Yenteel's tortured breath caught in his throat and he made a noise.

"Don't try to talk," she said.

Then his eyes opened and he stared at her. He tried to speak again. His free arm reached out and grabbed her shoulder. She felt herself beginning to cry and cursed herself. This was not the time.

"Break."

The word was forced from him and she could see the concentration on his face as he made his failing body obey.

"Break?"

His eyes rolled up into their sockets and the lids closed. He slumped. Gally appeared on the other side of Shingul's neck. His face mirrored his concern—he was incapable of any duplicity. He was sad because there was something to be sad about.

"What did he mean?" said Kantees. "Break what?"

"Arrow," said Gally as if it was the most obvious thing in the world.

Kantees looked. Yes, the arrow, but break it where? Then she realised if it was broken between his arm and his stomach they would be able to move him more easily.

"Hold him so he doesn't fall."

Gally took hold of Yenteel's other arm and his leg, while Shingul continued to remain perfectly still, lying flat on the ground so that the injured man could be reached easily. It was astonishing how considerate the *ziri* seemed to be, but this was no time to be thinking about it.

This was going to hurt.

She took hold of the arrow where it pierced his side. His blood made it slick. Then placed her other hand on the shaft further out, beyond where it had entered his arm.

It's only an arrow, she thought. *Easy to break.*

Trying to keep her right hand still she pushed back with the other. Yenteel's fingers twitched as the shaft bent, taking his arm with it. He groaned. She knew she wasn't keeping the arrow rigid and it was moving inside him.

She yelled and shoved hard. The wood snapped. Yenteel moaned as the pain ripped through him. She released her hands and the wood shifted back into position. They had to move him off Shingul's back and that would hurt too.

If only one of them were a healer and could repair the damage that was being done.

But wishing was riding a *ziri*. Except she had done that.

There was still no healer here, the best she could do was hope the damage was not too great and he would recover. She let Gally take the weight since he was strong and he was on the side without the arrow. She pushed Yenteel's leg over Shingul's neck and together she and Gally laid him on the ground.

Shingul sat back on her haunches, leaning on her wing joints, and brought her head round. She sniffed at Yenteel and opened her jaws. For one terrifying moment Kantees thought the *ziri* was going to take a bite out of him, just like one of the animal carcasses. But instead her tongue emerged and she licked him.

Tasting the blood, thought Kantees. She knelt down beside Yenteel and pushed Shingul's massive head away. The man was breathing and though each breath was shallow the rhythm was steady.

She wondered what she should do next. There were horror stories about people who died of injuries when there was no healer nearby. Or were allowed to die of injuries even if there was a healer available. They would lose their blood and die, or their bodies simply ceased to function. Sometimes they would rot like dead meat while they still lived.

She shuddered at the thought. It seemed the damage was not great enough for him to simply die, but he had lost a lot of blood—Shingul was now busy cleaning her feathers of it—so there was the risk he would rot from the inside. And that was the worst prospect of all.

"Gally, take the saddles off the *ziri*."

"No chains."

"I know, but we must trust them not to fly away."

"Romain say Gally not trusted."

"I trust you Gally, and the *ziri* trust you. Looesa let you ride, and put his head down for you, didn't he?"

"I ride Looesa," he said and she could tell from his voice he was smiling.

"Yes you did, as good as a master. Now get the saddles off them, they have flown hard and for a long time. They need to rest."

"All right, Kantees," he said as if she had been scolding him, then went off to where the dark shape of Sheesha watched them.

She turned her attention back to Yenteel. There was not enough light in the sky to see what she could do about the wounds. So they would have to wait until morning.

What could she do?

She fetched her bag and pulled out the stone water bottle. It was heavy but she preferred it to skins. There was a stream nearby, she had seen it as they descended.

"Gally, stay with the *ziri*. I'm going to fetch water."

"Gally is thirsty," said Gally.

Kantees smiled humourlessly and headed for the trees. Behind her there was a grunt from a *ziri* and she heard one of them following her. She wasn't going to argue, she had never been out in the open after dark, and alone, before. She had lived all her life in relative safety, first in the town house and then in the castle tower.

There were animals out here in the wild that could kill you in a moment. Having a *zirichak* at her shoulder would probably dissuade all but the biggest.

The ground got muddy before she reached the river. Then her foot got caught on a submerged root and she almost went over. She was rapidly coming to the conclusion that she did not like the outside. Stone walls, a fire, and a troop of armsmen for protection were much more attractive.

Then her other foot went into cold running water and a bed of soft mud. She took the stopper from the bottle and dipped it below the water. She heard the bubbles coming from it—then the lapping of the water by a giant tongue. Sheesha was drinking. It seemed he had no problem being out in the open at night.

Kantees drank from the bottle first. It made her cold all the way down. Then she refilled it and made her muddy way back to where Yenteel lay. Gally had finished removing the saddles so she told him to lead Looesa and Shingul down to the river to drink.

"And be careful," she said. "It's very muddy. Your feet could get stuck or you might fall over and get it everywhere."

"All right, Kantees. Come on, Looesa. Come on, Shingul." He said it exactly the way Kantees did. This time she did smile and felt happier. He seemed to be coping with the new situation better than she was, but then he didn't have to worry about a dying man, or being chased, or trying to find Jelamie, or being strung up as an escaped slave. No healer could bring you back from *that* journey.

When she was satisfied he was heading the right way, with the *ziri* following him, she turned her attention back to Yenteel. She found one of the saddles and managed to prop his head up. Then she opened the bottle and touched it against his mouth. Nothing. She frowned and tipped it up until the water dribbled down the sides of his cheeks. Still there was no response.

"Come on, Yenteel, drink," she said and peeled back his upper lip with her free hand while trying to pour the water in his mouth.

This time he reacted and she could feel, rather than see, him swallowing. She felt pleased with herself, gave him time to deal with that mouthful of water, and went through the process again until the bottle was empty. She did not think she had lost too much.

Let him take that into his body.

A wave of fatigue ran through her and she almost passed out as she knelt beside him. Sheesha nudged her and she fell backwards.

"What was that for?" she said but Sheesha did not make any noise. And she could not see what he was doing. "We have to wait for the others to get back."

It did not take long before Gally and the *ziri* returned, but in the meanwhile she was getting cold. The tension that had shielded her was wearing off. She had relaxed and with that came the exhaustion.

They had no shelter. She looked across to Sheesha who, as the others returned, curled himself up into his sleeping position. Looesa did the same but Shingul went to where Yenteel lay, placed herself along his length, and covered him with her wing.

In the dark they melded into one mass of shadow but still Kantees stared. Shingul was protecting Yenteel and keeping him warm. Like a mother. Like the mother Kantees had never known. Her eyes became moist once more and she sniffed to clear the sensation.

"Time for bed, Gally."

"My bed is far."

"Yes it is, so you will have a new bed."

"You have a new bed?"

"Looesa is your bed."

"Looesa?"

Kantees found his hand in the dark and led him to where the *zirichak* had curled up. Still huge despite that.

"Ask him if you can sleep under his wing," said Kantees.

"Gally sleep under your wing, Looesa?"

There was no movement.

"Just push a little bit, just there." She took his hand and laid it on Looesa's neck. The *ziri* moved, opened up a little, and lifted his wing. Gally needed no further prompting and carefully climbed inside the space. Shingul adjusted and the wing came down.

"'Night, Gally."

"'Night, Kantees. 'Night Looesa."

The *ziri* grunted. Kantees shook her head in wonderment. It was less as if they were simple animals, and more as if they were friends. Well, of course, she understood that, she had been with Sheesha so long that he was a friend. But the way Shingul was treating Yenteel, whom she had never met, did not make sense.

Sheesha made a low growling noise, not aggressive.

"Yes, all right, Sheesha, I'm coming."

She turned and found him waiting with his wing raised.

"I don't understand," she said quietly but Sheesha was already snoring.

It was fine for him to go to sleep immediately, he did not have her worries. Even though she was so tired it took her a long time to sleep as their options—or lack of them—went through her mind.

They needed to keep moving but Yenteel's injury made that impossible.

One thing at a time was the last thought she remembered having as the warmth of Sheesha's feathers drew her into sleep.

12

How big is Esternes?

She woke up with that question in her mind. She had asked it once when she had been at the town house, and been struck to the floor for the impertinence. Her master at that time had not been a rich man, and he was a scholar. They lived by the sea in Dakastown although she did not get the opportunity to go out much. She spent most of her time cleaning.

But just because she was cleaning did not mean that she did not have ears. The scholar was consulted for his wisdom and his astronomical predictions. This was a tricky area because such things were traditionally the province of the patterners. They kept their knowledge to themselves for the most part.

The scholar knew he was walking a fine line but he always managed to keep to the right side of it. He did not trespass on the territory of the patterners. As far as Kantees knew he had never made a pattern in all the time she was with him. It was said that true skill with patterning required one be born with the talent and train with it for years. There were rumours of wild talent, but Kantees could not ask, she could only listen and learn.

Except for that one day when the master had been looking at his maps. Someone had asked him a question and paid their money. She did not know what the question was, all she was doing was cleaning the grate. And the question popped into her head. She knew that Esternes was an island but she did not know how big. Just as the question popped into her head, it popped out of her mouth. In reply the master had knocked her to the ground.

Her duties then kept her to the kitchen and the garden. Shortly thereafter she was sold.

All for a question.

Romain did not like her asking questions either. He preferred to dictate his wisdom in regard to the *zirichasa* for her to absorb. But she did have questions and sometimes they were things he had failed to mention, so he could be angry at her ignorance but he still had to answer her.

As time passed she learnt everything he had to offer and he simply repeated himself for he seemed incapable of remembering what it was he had told her. When Gally joined them it worked out for the best because it meant that he could lecture Gally who definitely did forget, or completely failed to understand. So Romain could repeat himself as much as he wished.

He ceased to instruct Kantees but she still had questions and there was no one to ask.

The day was bright, the air was cold, and there was dew on the ground. The cold did not bother her but it could not be good for Yenteel. She stepped out from the enfolding wings of Sheesha and stretched. Behind her she heard Sheesha doing the same and the broad shadow of his wings was draped across the ground.

Looesa stood up, and dropped Gally to the ground before stretching. Only Shingul remained where she was, still with her wing across Yenteel.

Kantees sighed. She was still tired but the brightness of the day drove the sleep from her. She found the water bottle.

"Gally, go to the river, fill this, and bring it back."

"I am hungry, Kantees."

"I am too, Gally, but we must look after Yenteel first."

"Why?"

"He is hurt and ill. Fetch the water for him."

Gally grumbled but he went, followed by Looesa, and when Kantees knelt beside Yenteel, Shingul stood up and went after them. Some birds went about in flocks, Kantees knew, so perhaps *zirichasa* did as well. It was a question she could not answer, just as she did not know the size of Esternes.

Yenteel's colour looked bad in daylight but her concern was the broken pieces of arrow. Perhaps she should deal with this now, before Gally came back. She preferred to protect him from the more unpleasant parts of their adventure.

With her knife she cut away the cloth of Yenteel's jacket and shirt. It seemed a shame because they were of excellent quality. Whoever his master was, he dressed Yenteel well.

The arrow had pierced the lower arm and it was not as bad as she feared. It had gone deep enough to hit a muscle but she did not think it had hit the bone beneath. Looking at the broken arrow she could see that pulling it back out was a bad idea since the break was full of broken bits of wood. It would tear his skin.

Carefully she brought his arm back and away from his body, then placed a knee on his hand and held his arm just above the arrow. She took hold of the broken end and pulled. The fact that Yenteel shuddered with the pain as she drew the wood through his arm pleased her —at least he could still feel pain. He was still in there.

It did not take long before the arrow's flights disappeared into him and then reappeared red with blood. Using the cloth she had cut off she made a bandage around the wounds. They seeped blood a little but it was not serious.

She was shocked when Yenteel's other hand suddenly grabbed her shoulder. His eyes were wide. "When you take it out. You must burn it."

She heard the words but she did not understand them. It must have been clear in her face, as he panted, "Your knife. Make it hot, very hot, when you take out the arrow. Burn the skin shut. Seal it. Otherwise infection and bleeding. You understand?"

His grip was like a *ziri*'s talon digging in to her. She nodded even though she did not know what 'infection' was. "I understand."

He let go and fell back. "Do it now, or I die."

She stared at his face and then at the wound at his side. He had lost consciousness again but she whispered, "I'll try."

Gally was returning and presented her with the water bottle.

"Find wood, Gally," she said. "This is important. We must make a fire as quick as we can. The hottest fire we can."

"I'm tired."

"Please, Gally, don't be difficult. The hottest fire we can."

The *ziri* did not seem at all concerned by the fire that Kantees now had raging. She had built a small wall from earth and filled it with tinder as Gally fetched larger sticks. She got it alight with her tinderbox and kept it going long enough to dry out the twigs, which in turn dried out the branches Gally collected. The wall kept the heat in and the wind out. At least, she wasn't completely useless.

Once she was satisfied, she took a straight branch, tied the knife to its end with Yenteel's boot straps and placed it into the fire.

"We have to take the arrow out, Gally, but we must stop all the bleeding and to do that Yenteel says we must burn his skin."

"That will hurt him," said Gally. "Bad."

"Yes it will, but he told me I must do it. If we don't he will die."

"I like Yenteel."

Kantees wasn't sure she did, she barely knew him, and besides Gally liked almost everyone including those who were cruel to him— simply because he did not understand their taunts and tricks.

"Yes, and that's why we have to do this. But you have to help me."

"Help Kantees?"

"Yes, you have to hold him. It will hurt when I take the arrow out, and it will hurt when I burn him. He will move and you have to hold him still otherwise it will be harder to help him."

It took a few more attempts to convince Gally that all this really would help even though it was like doing a bad thing.

But in the end they could not delay any longer. The fire was hot. The blade wasn't glowing, but it was as hot as she could manage.

She had Gally kneel on Yenteel's shoulders. And she put her knee on his hand again. There wasn't much she could do about his legs, she would just have to be quick. Thankfully she knew that the castle archers did not use barbed heads. It should come straight out, though she guessed there was a hands-length of wood and iron in Yenteel's belly.

She closed her eyes and took a deep breath. She did not want to do this. She might kill him, but if she didn't do it he would die anyway and that would also be her fault.

Her eyes open once more, she smiled at Gally.

"Ready?"

He nodded seriously.

Kantees took hold of the end of the arrow. She had cleaned it of blood and bound it with another bootstrap, so her hand would not slip. She had her other hand on the branch with the knife at its end.

"Three … two … one … now."

The arrow seemed stuck at first; she pulled harder and it came free. Yenteel squirmed and moaned with the pain. The shaft's bloodied length slid out and dark blood flowed from the wound. She dropped the arrow, lifted the knife, and with both hands, prepared to press the flat against the hole in Yenteel's side.

It was such a small hole. She hesitated. Romain would always sew up injuries to the *ziri*. Blood leaked from his side but it did not pump. She always had a needle and thread with her because Romain would check on her.

"Kantees?" said Gally.

She threw the knife away from her and it hissed in the grass, sending up tiny embers.

"Fetch my bag, Gally, by Sheesha's saddle. Quick."

She could sew the two sides together and it would heal as it should. If she burned him it would make a terrible scar and she could not be sure it would heal properly. Then she could bind him around the middle and it would help to hold the wound shut. If he rotted from the inside, it would happen regardless of what method she used to mend him.

Gally returned and she found the needle leather and the thread. It was strong and would not break easily. She had Gally hold him still while she poked the iron needle into him. It was like mending a hole in clothes. The skin was tougher but it worked the same way. And it did not take long. Romain was good for something then.

Yenteel was so far gone that he did not react to the pricking; she wondered whether that would have been true if she had burned him. No, this was far better.

Rummaging through Yenteel's bag she found a shirt. It wasn't clean but it would do. She used it as a pad over the injury and wrapped cording several times around him to hold it in place. It would have to do.

She looked up.

The day had barely progressed. It was not even midday. The sky was clear save for a few slow-moving clouds that seemed intent on avoiding the sun. The air remained cold but it was warm in the light.

She sat back exhausted.

Yenteel was resting quietly and his breathing was steady though still shallow. Gally sat beside him holding his hand.

The *ziri* were lying together with their long necks on the ground but Sheesha had his eyes open, looking at her across his flat snout.

"I've done everything I can," she said as if he could understand her. "It's up to the Mother now."

Then her stomach growled and Sheesha glanced at her midriff accusingly. It made her laugh inside. The *zirichak* pushed himself up with his wings and sat back on his haunches. He put his head on its side to look at her.

"You're hungry?" she said. "It's good for you. Can't have you getting fat."

Sheesha gave a short calling bark and the other two lifted their heads. They looked in the direction of the mountains—shadowy and blue in the sunlight with their tips glowing white.

"No, Sheesha!" Kantees stumbled to her feet. This was his take-off pose.

He glanced briefly in her direction and then launched himself up. The downdraught from his wings buffeted her. Then Looesa went up as well. They wheeled in a spiral gaining height with deep and powerful beats of their wings.

They were beautiful with their feathers shimmering in iridescent blues and greens as the sun's light reflected off them. Sheesha's turn faced him towards the mountains and he shot away with Looesa in a perfect position to the right and behind.

Kantees could do nothing but despair. She watched until the dots they became in the distance were indistinguishable from the dots her eyes invented.

He's gone.

13

She brought her attention back to their meagre camp. Gally still sat with Yenteel, and Shingul still lay on the grass. Was she all right? But she had no reason to think there was anything wrong with the *ziri*.

Why hadn't she gone with the males?

Kantees forced herself to calm. They must be coming back otherwise she would have gone.

Surely that must be true?

Gally was unconcerned but that was hardly surprising, he only worried about the small things. And he worried about Kantees. Keeping the secret of having seen her must have been difficult for him. As far as she knew he did not lie. So to be forced to keep silent must have been difficult.

She went back to where Yenteel lay and crouched down on the other side of him to Gally who was fiddling with something.

"I wanted to thank you, Gally," she said. He did not react but played with what looked like a smooth stone. Perhaps he picked it up at the stream. "I wanted to thank you for keeping my secret about riding Sheesha."

He said nothing.

"If anybody asks now, you can tell them, it's not a secret any more."

"They hurt Kantees?"

"Not for that, Gally," she said. "After what I've done now, stealing the *ziri*, they will punish me for that instead."

"Sheesha not stolen."

She smiled. "What would you call it then?"

"Sheesha helping."

"But Sheesha, Looesa, and Shingul are just animals, Gally," she said. "They just do as they're told." She looked in the direction that Sheesha had gone. "Well, when they want to, anyway."

Gally had gone back to the round stone. The sun glinted on it and she realised it was flat as well as round.

"What's that?"

"Mine. I found it."

"I know but can I have a look?"

"Gally's coin."

"I promise I will give it back," she said. "It looks very pretty, you could just come over here and show it to me if you don't trust me to touch it."

Which was a dirty trick and she felt bad about it the moment the words came out. It was the sort of thing Daybian would say to manipulate people.

Gally looked at her dubiously and then stretched out his arm across Yenteel's body. Rather than take it, Kantees held out her palm so he could decide to give it. It dropped heavily into her hand.

It was a coin and not small. Heavy too. It must be valuable. She had never had money; as a slave she was not allowed to own anything. Everyone broke the rule of course, but with small things that could be hidden easily—though their main currency was secrets.

Back in the tower she had one of Sheesha's feathers. They were supposed to hand them all in to be made into saleable items by people in the town—so they had value. But she had kept that one. Another crime to add to the list she would no doubt be punished for. Death would be too easy. No doubt there would be torture first to make sure she fully understood her crimes.

She shook her head and tried to escape the morbid thoughts.

It was not that she didn't know what coins looked like. She had seen enough of them changing hands in the gambling at the races. But they were always of dark metal and very small, some of them tiny. She had never seen one like this.

It had a man's face on one side. He looked like a Taymalin and he had some sort of circlet on his head, perhaps a king or lord. The other side showed the image of a *nachak* just from the waist up, depicting only its cruel upper arms, its torso, and head. Who would have the symbol of a *nachak*? They were vicious night hunters, so the stories went, and very big.

Not that she knew how big, there were stories that they were the size of a house. Some of the armsmen claimed to have seen them but who knew if they were telling the truth.

She stared at the coin and tilted it until it reflected the sun.

At a guess this would probably be enough to buy a dozen slaves like her. Or enough food to keep her fed for a year. She looked up and smiled at Gally who had a concerned look on his face. She tossed it back; he caught it and gave her a relieved grin.

Then it dawned on her. "Gally, where did you find it?"

He pointed to the river.

"Show me."

The words were hardly out of her mouth when she remembered Yenteel, lying there directly in front of her. She was annoyed at him for being like this. She stood up anyway.

"Shingul?"

The female was facing away from them and towards the mountains, but she lifted her head and bent her neck back to look at them.

"Look after Yenteel, please." She pointed down at his unconscious body.

Shingul grunted in a way that implied she understood, although that was impossible, then went back to watching the mountains. Kantees shook her head. The *ziri* were confusing, on the one hand they could not be more than animals, and yet they seemed to understand.

"Show me the way, Gally."

They set off with Kantees puzzling over the *ziri*. People in the town kept *zatesa* as pets and to guard property. They were quite clever and could be trained or learn tricks. But *zirichasa* were bigger. Did that mean they were cleverer?

They approached the stream. Gally made to go straight through the mud.

"Let's go round," said Kantees pointing to the side away from the woods. A coarse thick grass grew in the mud but she could see the cropped grass closer to the water further along.

Gally stopped and looked obstinate. She had asked him where he had found the coin and that's where he wanted to go.

"Was it on this side of the stream?" she asked.

"Other side."

"That's why you were so wet."

"Fell over."

"I know," she said. "If it's the other side we can go round."

It also looked as if the channel was narrower there. She headed round and, still reluctant, dragging his feet, Gally followed.

The stream here could be jumped easily. It had cut into the ground, running deep and fast, before it opened out and pooled in the area before the trees. She had not noticed before but the ground dropped off on the other side of the trees.

It was then she noticed the grass on this side was ripped up. Something had dug into the ground and torn huge holes into it but only over an area that—*was exactly the size of the giant tekrak*. She walked around the churned-up area. The *tekrak* had come down here, landed and dug its roots into the ground, just like the small ones did.

They had camped here.

She looked round and found three firepits. The ground was disturbed here as well but not in the same way. She was no tracker but it was clear people had made fires and cooked. There were even a few bones about the place. A blanket, damp and torn, lay close to the trees. But if only she had been a tracker she might know how long they had stayed, how far behind them she was.

It was enough to lift her heart.

Something pulled at her sleeve. Gally.

"Gally show Kantees."

"Yes, of course, sorry."

She let him lead the way back towards the stream. It was less muddy on this side, because the land was a little higher, and there was a low bank where the ground fell away to the water.

Gally leaned over and pointed. Then he toppled into the water. Kantees was there in a moment. Gally was on his knees pulling at something in the water, partially covered by the mud; it was a body face down in the water. Gally splashed about, his feet sinking deeper trying to pull the body up.

Kantees laid her hand on his shoulder. "Gally, stop."

"Help him, Kantees. We have to help the master."

"It's too late, Gally. He's dead."

The boy stopped, released the clothing and stood up straight. "Dead?"

"He's been there since the raiders stayed here. A few days. He's dead."

"Sorry, sire." Gally's words were directed at the submerged body.

Kantees gave a sad smile. "I'm sure he'd be happy you tried to save him."

"Gally did try to save him."

"You did."

"But he's dead."

"Yes."

"What do we do, Kantees?"

Good question. He must have come with the raiders, so perhaps there was a clue to who they were on him. The mud had all but claimed him and after a few days in the water she did not relish what his face would look like. She could see one of his hands and that was white, bloated and torn where something had taken bites out of him.

But if there were any clues she needed to know them.

It took a long time to get him out. It seemed that he had been sinking slowly and the mud wanted to keep him. It clung and sucked at him. Both Kantees and Gally were soaked and filthy by the time they forced the water to give him up.

Finally they had him on the higher bank and water seeped from him.

She was surprised that his face was not as bad as she had expected. It was bloated but had not been chewed. In fact all the skin that had been stuck in the mud was untouched. The exposed parts, however, were a different matter.

All manner of tiny water insects and little crawlers—even small fish—made their escape as the body was brought out. Even now she could see he was covered in them. They were probably inside as well.

She wanted to let him dry out in the sun a little, but as soon as he did he would start to smell and that would attract all manner of creatures. They might be able to deal with, or scare off, some of them, but there was a limit.

So she searched him.

He had been rich. The clothes were of better quality than the Jakalain wore. She took his shoes, which would be usable when they dried. With Gally's help she got his jacket off. If he had a money pouch, that was gone. The coin must have been his. She doubted that one coin—that could feed her for a year—would have paid for his clothes.

The only other thing she was interested in was how he had died but there was no indication on his body. No blows that she could see, and no stab wounds. Perhaps they had just held his head in the water until he drowned. But if he had been murdered, why had they taken his money but not his clothes?

She shook her head. The Taymalin had strange customs. Who knew what they were thinking?

Flies were already becoming a nuisance around the body. Kantees looked around a little worriedly. It must be well past midday now, and she was getting very hungry. Something caught her eye and she jerked her head round. She was certain there had been a movement in the trees.

The afternoon was getting warm. He would rot even faster. What little wind there was would be carrying the scent out across the plain. She knew there were no large animals near the Jakalain castle, but they were not near it any more. There could even be *nachasa*.

"Let's go," she said and set off back the way they had come, carrying the coat and boots. If Yenteel recovered he might be able to tell them more.

Once across the stream she glanced back. Half a dozen creatures loped out of the trees and stopped. They were being cautious, checking the skies and all around as they moved, but they were going straight for the body.

That he was going to get eaten did not bother Kantees. It was just nature. She was more concerned about how she was going to deal with her own hunger. Even if she had a weapon, other than a knife, she had no idea how to hunt or set traps.

She might be able to start a fire but she knew nothing of survival in the wild.

14

Shingul had moved while they had been away and was back with Yenteel, lying alongside him with her wing across his body. Unlike the way she had placed it on his body in the night, this time she had it arched to shade him from the sun.

Kantees went back to the stream and refilled the water bottle after quenching her own thirst. Gally, in the meantime, was going through Shingul's feathers looking for bugs. She could probably leave him to do the simple tasks. He was used to them and they still needed to be done.

Yenteel's skin was cold despite the warmth of the day. She knew that could not be a good sign. He drank the water she offered him in an unthinking reaction, for his body knew what to do even though he did not wake up. He only lost half the bottle's contents, so he took in a good amount.

She untied the bandages and pads covering his wounds. Each of the three wounds was red and leaking a transparent fluid, but the inflamed areas did not seem to have spread so she was happy with that. And although he did not wake, his breathing seemed to have settled to a slower and deeper pace.

She could not be sure but she thought perhaps he might not die.

"Thank you for looking after him, Shingul," she said. The *ziri* raised her head and neck and turned back to look at the girl. Her eyes were wide apart on her head but lidded like a person's, not like some of the smaller creatures.

Kantees' time with the scholar had taught her that there were several classes of creatures but that they could be divided into two main groups: the ones that resembled people in their skeletons, their skin, and their blood, and those that resembled the *Slissac*. The two major divisions had groups within them, but it started to get complicated and she was never able to hear enough to explain it.

She had heard enough to know that the *zirichasa* were on the *Slissac* side but that did not stop her side using them. People rode *kichesa* on the ground, and there were horses too. Though not many of either on Esternes as far as she knew.

Then there was the other complication. While humans—and the *Slissac*, if any still existed—could perform magic through the use of patterns, there were creatures that had magic woven into their very being. The *tekrasa*, for example, with their fire-tubes and the gas in them that let them rise into the air even though they were only plants. Or the wolves that never made a sound yet moved like a single creature as if they were joined in their minds.

She looked at Shingul. The *ziri* had no built-in magic. At least she did not think so, as Romain had never spoken of it. They were clever and understood a lot, but no magic. They simply loved to fly as fast as possible.

A booming call sounded across the wilderness, deep and loud and seeming to go right through her. Shingul raised her head and called back in the same voice. Kantees had never heard them make a sound like that. She did not even know they could.

She stood and, squinting against the brightness, scanned the skies.

Shingul boomed again, this time it was a sequence of three short calls that she kept repeating every few moments.

Then another boom from the sky. Kantees saw a dot that resolved rapidly into two and then they had wings and were gliding down fast. Shingul was looking the same way and stopped her booming.

As the two *ziri* closed in and grew in size she saw that both of them carried something in their claws. And the somethings had legs and heads dangling limply. Her mouth watered and she turned to the fire. It was still hot and the embers glowed. She added more tinder, which was instantly consumed in flames, so she switched to twigs and a couple of smaller branches.

A shadow went over followed by thumps as two dead animals hit the ground: They must have found a wild herd of *kelukisa* and picked off a couple of young ones. She was not experienced with preparing meat to eat, but she knew the basics, and having a stream nearby was useful.

The necks of both animals were broken and there were claw marks in the bodies where they had been carried.

Sheesha and Looesa landed nearby and waddled over, nowhere near as elegant on the ground as in the air. Sheesha picked up the carcass furthest from Kantees and dropped it in front of Shingul who put a wing claw on the body, clamped her jaws on a leg and ripped it off.

Kantees picked up her knife and set to work on the other body.

It took a long time to get enough of the skin off to be able to hack at the muscle. She put one whole leg over the fire, then spent more time chopping one of the other legs into much smaller pieces which she draped on sticks next to the flame in the hope they would cook faster. She set Gally to watch them. He was as hungry as she was but they were not so far gone as to eat raw meat.

She noticed that Sheesha and Looesa allowed Shingul to eat as much of the other as she wanted. Then they finished it off between them. They did not argue but Looesa always let Sheesha take his portion first. Perhaps they had eaten when they had been away.

Was this normal behaviour? She had no idea. Most animals in her experience, and that included other Kadralin, would consume as much as they could before letting another eat, if they had a choice. The *zirichasa* seemed quite civilised—and thoughtful, since they had brought back food for everyone.

The meat was delicious. Perhaps more so because of their hunger.

Kantees kept the fire up and roasted the haunch. She took the remains of the carcass to the stream and set about removing the innards. It was a disgusting process that turned the water all manner of unpleasant colours.

She glanced at where the body of the dead man had been laid. No one had moved him since, and she was glad she was not too close. The *chakisa*-like creatures were still ripping their way through his flesh and innards with little screeches of anger as they fought over some tidbit or another.

There were several smaller ones squatting on their tails making a loose circle, waiting to dash in and grab something. The ones on her side noticed what was happening in the water and investigated. Once they realised there was food here they jumped into the water and gobbled up the parts she was discarding.

Back in the castle it was forbidden to feed the *chakisa* that infested the place, because they ate the bugs and smaller creatures and would not do their job if they were not hungry. These creatures were like them but twice the size.

Kantees did not notice at first, since she was focused on the carcass, but when she looked up they were closer. Perhaps half a dozen of them. And they were watching her.

When her knife went into the carcass and the remains floated away they would leap on them, arguing and snapping with their little pointed teeth. But then they were closer again.

One of them ran a few steps closer, its little feet splashing through the water.

Kantees suddenly felt unsafe. It might be that she could stop one of them, perhaps even two, but six or seven could take her down even if they did not even come up to her knees. Then there was a sound behind her. She turned her head slowly. Another one.

Only a short distance away were the fire, Gally, and three *zirichasa* for whom these things would be barely a mouthful.

She suspected that if she abandoned the food they would ignore her, but she was unwilling to give in to these little bullies. She took hold of the leg of the remains and stood up, which sent them scurrying back a few paces. Since she had stripped out the innards what was left was much lighter.

"Sheesha," she said, not loudly but enough that her voice would carry.

His head popped up and he looked in her direction. The movement did not escape the ones in front of her; every one of those little heads turned towards the camp. They did not move; the threat was too far away to distract them from the food they thought they could get.

Then she heard the flop and thump of a big wing moving.

The little creatures scattered, including the one behind her that zipped past. Their movement attracted the attention of the others eating the dead man. They saw Sheesha and responded by fleeing back into the woods.

Kantees gave a short laugh and dragged the remains back to the camp where she put the rest of it on and in the fire to cook.

"That smells good," said Yenteel in a voice that could barely be heard.

15

*K*antees was surprised at how relieved she was when Yenteel woke up. He gratefully accepted more water and he seemed able to use his undamaged arm. His colour looked better and his skin seemed more alive.

She cut a piece of meat into tiny pieces, so he did not have to chew, and fed them to him.

Shingul moved away and went to the pool with Looesa. They went in and splashed about, almost as if they were having fun although Kantees assumed they were just cleaning themselves. Seeing the *ziri* like this made her realise how little she knew about them, really—how little Romain or any of the other keepers knew.

Having eaten and drunk, Yenteel went back to sleep.

She had hoped to talk to him about the dead body, and she was becoming concerned about pursuit. It was true that no one would be flying to catch them—they would have succeeded already—but, while a *ziri* could fly fast, if they stayed where they were someone would catch up with them eventually.

Especially if they followed the smoke from the fire. Kantees looked in horror at the rising column. It must be visible for miles. She poured what was left of the water onto it, then ran down to the stream to get more.

She paused only long enough to fill the bottle—noticing that Looesa and Shingul were preening each other while sitting in the water and stirring up the mud.

It took another bottle to put the fire out completely. Gouts of steam were rising but they dissipated quickly.

Then Sheesha boomed. Kantees looked where he was looking, back the way they had come, and saw a growing patch of dark against the sky. A booming call echoed back. Kantees shook her head. It was too late. She had been away only a day and it was already too late. Someone had found her.

The *ziri* went into a spiral, descending fast.

Who could ride that well? Who would decide to do it? There was only one answer and she knew it before she even saw his face. Daybian. And he was riding old Jintan. Kantees was surprised the beast could do it. She wished he had not been able.

As the *ziri* spiralled in for a final landing, she fetched her knife and put it in her belt at the small of her back so Daybian would not see it.

Then, before she could think to stop him, Gally ran up to the landing *ziri* and took the reins just as he would have back at the castle. She had thought to call it home, but it was not that any longer.

"So, at least one person here still knows how to respect their masters."

Daybian unbuckled himself and slipped down to the ground. His movements were smooth, with no sign he had been in the saddle too long.

He peeled off his riding gloves. There was a short sword at his waist but he did not go for it. Kantees did not know what to say. She felt crushed and broken, her life now numbered in days.

Sheesha had watched the arrival and now moved so that he stood beside and slightly behind Kantees. It was a comfort to have him there even though there was nothing he could do—he had no under-standing of the situation beyond perhaps her feeling of unease.

Daybian's eyes narrowed as he followed Sheesha's movement but even so he walked forward. The fire stood between them still smoking slightly, she must have missed some embers after all.

"Am I really that ugly?" said Daybian.

Kantees could not help herself. "*What?*"

He shook his head. "No respect at all."

"I cannot commit any greater crime than I already have," she said. "I do not need to show you any respect."

"It might go better for you at a trial if you did."

"Death is death, *sire*." She twisted the last word with as much sarcasm as she could muster.

"Regardless," he said. "My original question still stands."

"I didn't understand it."

"You hit me over the head with Sheesha's shit shovel, just because I wanted to lie with you. I did not think I was so ugly that you would feel the need to do that to escape me."

"Are you so selfish?" she said. "Nothing I did was about you."

"So you don't think I'm ugly?"

"It's not relevant."

"It is to me."

Kantees closed her eyes. She found it hard to believe she was having this conversation. "Whatever the merits of your appearance —" He smiled. "—or the lack of them—" The smile vanished. "—how can I make you understand that I hit you over the head because you insisted on being present when I wanted to escape?"

"You're saying it's a coincidence."

Kantees opened her mouth. The conversation was getting so mixed up she was not entirely sure what the right answer was.

"It was a coincidence that you desired to force yourself on me at a time when I was planning to escape, yes."

"That's all right then."

"Is it?"

"Yes."

"You rode Jintan all the way out here after me because your pride had been pricked?"

"It wasn't the only reason."

"That makes it so much better," she said. "You've come to take me back. I won't go and I will fight you if you try to make me. I would rather die here than be forced to return."

It seemed it was Daybian's turn to look confused. "Not at all."

"I have committed several capital crimes," she said, "including hitting you over the head."

"I believe we have dealt with that issue."

"If you're not here to take me back, and you're satisfied your pride hasn't been injured, why are you here?"

"To help you search for my brother, of course."

At which point Kantees felt faint and leaned back against Sheesha.

"But you can't. You don't have the right to forgive my crimes."

"We'll worry about that later," he said. "That meat smells good, fetch me some, will you? Is the water in that stream clean? And who is that fellow lying on the ground? He doesn't look well."

She did not fetch him any meat—he could get his own, which he did—but she did assure him that the stream was clean enough to drink from, upstream of where she had cleaned out the carcass. That information came with a warning that he should watch out for the big *chakisa*, especially in groups of three or more.

Yenteel woke up again as the sun was descending. He took some more food and water. He was stronger which made Kantees a lot happier.

"Lord Daybian is here."

Yenteel raised an eyebrow. "He has not killed you or taken you back."

Since that was obviously true, and Yenteel had not expressed it as a question, she said nothing more.

"What does he want?"

"To help me find his brother."

"I said he'd be trouble. Do you trust him?"

"Of course not, he's one of the masters. He tried ordering me about as soon as he arrived."

Yenteel glanced across at where Daybian was watching the sun go down and scratching his behind. "He does not strike me as being very bright."

"He isn't," she said. "But he's a good rider, and if you can believe what he says he knows how to use his sword."

"I thought that was what you were avoiding."

Kantees looked daggers at Yenteel, who had the ghost of a smile on his face. "You can feed yourself. You're obviously feeling better."

Then Yenteel said something in a language she did not understand. He had a look of hope on his face which dissolved when she shook her head.

"I don't understand."

"It is your language, Kantees," he said. "Of your people, the Kadralin."

"It is forbidden to speak it."

He made a slight movement that might have been a shrug.

"Why did you come to Jakalain?" she said. "Why were you looking for me? And don't say it was because the world's pattern told you to."

He gave a slight shake of his head. "It is a story that would be long in the telling. We need to be moving on."

"You're not strong enough."

"No, but I am strong enough to make a pattern or two with your help."

"You're a patterner?"

"Everyone can make patterns, Kantees. Everyone does even if they don't think they do. Every movement, every act, every spoken word is part of a pattern."

"But it's not magical."

"Isn't it? When a musician moves their hands on their instrument and it makes a tune, is that not a pattern that is magical?"

"But that's just … doing things right. I've heard plenty of tunes which were not done right."

"And that's the point."

She sighed. Clearly there was no way to argue with him. "What do you need?"

"Fetch my bag. There's some charcoal in a box, and if you can manage to find a cloth that I can draw on, it would help."

She brought the bag and located the box. Yenteel also possessed a white linen shirt so she brought that out and held it up in front of him. He sighed. "It'll wash out, I suppose."

He also wanted something flat to lean on, like a board, but that was harder to come by until Kantees saw Daybian's short sword flapping against his leg. He seemed to be quite content just staring into the distance. Perhaps that was sufficient to occupy his limited mind.

"I need to borrow your sword."

"To kill me?"

She ignored his comment. "Yenteel needs to do a patterning, and he needs something to rest the cloth on while he forms the patterns."

"That slave is a patterner?"

"Yes, apparently he is."

"It's forbidden for slaves to do magic."

"Yes, well, it's also forbidden to hit masters on the head with shit shovels, but you seem to have recovered from that."

Daybian unsheathed his sword. "Do not attempt to run me through with it."

"Much as it would give me great pleasure," said Kantees, "I will restrain myself. I don't hate you personally, Daybian."

"Then you might consider lying with me?"

"Can't you think with your head instead of what's between your legs?"

He grinned and opened his mouth. She cut him off.

"Just don't. Yenteel has already made that joke. It wasn't funny then, and it won't be funny now."

"He thought it too? Then perhaps I will like him after all." Daybian pulled out the sword. It was probably worth about two years' food to someone like her. For him it was just a serviceable tool for killing. It wasn't even of the best quality.

But it did have a flat surface. She took it back to Yenteel who told her to lay the cloth over it and hold it taut while he inscribed symbols. He hummed at the same time. Quite tunelessly.

The designs he made had lots of straight lines forming squares, triangles and other more complex shapes. It was a pattern, but she couldn't see any meaning in it. He took breaks as he worked; the light was failing but he seemed clear about what he was doing.

"Tie it next to my skin under the bandage," he said. "This mark must be over the wound." He pointed just before he passed out.

Kantees made a face but did as he asked. She needed to check his wound anyway.

The fire was going out. There was a shuddering in the air as one of the *ziri* launched into the air. It was Jintan.

"Gally?"

He emerged from the shadows between the others.

"What's Jintan doing?"

"He is going to have a shit."

"How do you know?"

"He was itchy."

"Itchy?"

"Jumping up and down a little bit, Kantees. Did you not want him to go? He would make a mess here and we don't have any shovels."

Kantees had never noticed Sheesha doing that. He seemed content to make a pile in the corner for her to clear up. It occurred to her that in some ways Sheesha was as arrogant as Daybian.

"No, that's all right," she said. "We don't want a mess here. He will come back?"

"Yes, Kantees."

"You keep looking after them then."

"Yes, Kantees, but there is not much to do. Romain will say Gally is lazy."

"Romain isn't here."

"No, Kantees."

Gally turned and went back to the *ziri* who were lying together a short distance away.

"He's a bright lad," said Daybian.

Compared to you? Yes, she thought. "You can have your sword back." She held it out and he took it, sliding it smoothly back into its sheath with a natural confidence that suggested perhaps he really did know what he was doing with it.

"Can you build up the fire?" she added.

"Me?"

Her anger at all the arrogant masters exploded. "Yes, you! You want to come with me, then you do what I say."

"I don't take orders from slaves."

"I'm *not* a slave any more. Out here we're equals. Oh, and in case you're making unwarranted assumptions, I'm riding Sheesha. You can stay on Jintan."

He was quiet for a few moments. "I will admit I do not really know about building up fires. It's not something I have had to do."

"There is wood drying next to the fire. You take some of the branches and put them on the fire. Not too much or you'll suffocate it and we'll run out."

"I see. I will give that a try."

"Good." She was slightly disappointed at how swiftly he had given in. She had been looking forward to shouting at him again.

He turned away and went to the fire. She thought for a moment he seemed sad, but she shrugged it off. Of course he felt sad: she wouldn't let him express his arrogance.

She turned back to Yenteel and carefully untied the cords that held the pad. It was red with fresh blood. Simply drawing the pattern must have been too much effort for him, and he had reopened the wound. She would have to make sure he did not do that again.

That meant more delay. If Daybian could find them, then someone else could. At least at night the smoke would be less visible and nobody would be flying.

She wrapped the patterned cloth around him ensuring the right marks were on the arrow wound. Then she bandaged him up again.

At least she could fly away on Sheesha if it became too much. Except that she couldn't leave them, especially not Gally.

16

When Yenteel woke again, the white moon, Lostimal, was shining in the black. He drank more water and chewed some meat. There was not enough light for her to tell whether he was suffering more than before. His voice seemed about the same.

"You placed the pattern?" he said.

"Just as you said, with the one you pointed out over the wound."

He did not reply immediately but tried to adjust his position and groaned in the effort.

"You can't do that," she said. "If you need to move, tell me. You started bleeding again and this isn't going to help." She glanced at where the wound was but it was impossible to see anything.

"I must do this," he said, his voice straining with the pain he had to be feeling. "I have held you up too long as it is."

"You didn't ask to get shot."

"No, but they gave me that honour anyway."

"We could just wait for you to heal," she said, putting a smile on her face, even though he couldn't see it.

"You're a good liar," he said. "I could have been convinced if I didn't know the truth."

She sighed. "What do you have to do?"

"Work a healer pattern, the one I've drawn on the cloth."

"How can I help?"

"Just hold my hands."

"How long is this going to take?"

"Do you have somewhere you need to be?"

Apart from rescuing someone I don't even care about? A person I have destroyed my whole life for because I told a few lies? Even as she thought it, she knew that was unfair. She had committed the first crime to save a castle full of people who had enslaved her race. She still wasn't sure why. She could have ignored Sheesha. *Couldn't I?*

"I want to know if I'd be better sitting or kneeling."

"Sit."

It was awkward. She ended up facing him, on his wounded side so that he did not have to stretch his injured arm.

His hands were cold. Or hers warm.

She was aware that Daybian was looking, but then why shouldn't he? There was nothing else happening.

Yenteel began a chant. She did not recognise the language but it was similar to the one he had used before to her. So that meant it was Kadralin. Was there no end to the crimes they would commit together? Forbidden language. Forbidden magic. She might not be invoking the pattern but she was certainly helping.

He had shut his eyes and his words came out slurred. She knew that magic required strength and energy. Would he kill himself in an attempt to heal? He had never fully answered the question of why he had been seeking her out.

His master wanted her. What did that mean?

Then her fingers tingled. It was like the feeling when an arm or leg that had gone to sleep began to recover. She worried. There were stories of creatures that fed on the life patterns of others and drained them for their own sustenance. Was Yenteel one of them? Had he been lying? Was this all a ploy so that she would give herself willingly?

She would rather give herself to Daybian.

She giggled. At first she thought it had been out loud but no one said anything. She was confused. The tingling had crept up her arms.

He was eating her alive.

But she suppressed the panic. It made no sense. He had not chosen to be struck by an arrow. He had almost bled to death. What creature would put itself in so much danger simply to have another meal?

There was a grunting noise above her.

Sheesha.

She had not heard him approach. If his head was over them, he must have come in very close indeed. She realised her eyes were closed too, even though she could see lights moving. Golden threads wove in and out. Periodically new ones would appear from the left or right, or top, or bottom, and dance among the strands already there.

Then she realised what she was seeing.

It was the pattern of the healing. Some of the shapes made by the threads were the same as the ones Yenteel had drawn—but much finer and more complex. And so many more of them, as if the drawn pattern was a simplified version.

The tingling had gone through her and reached down into her belly, just as it also went up to her head where it made a ring of prickles as if her hair were standing on end.

Then the pattern seemed to stop moving. The golden light faded from it but somehow she knew the working was not complete. She did not know what to do. Yenteel must have reached the limit of his strength but it had not been enough. She had to do something.

Why? And even as that word filtered through her mind, she knew it was just another part of her. That part that said she should not care about anyone else because no one cared about her. All she had to do was release Yenteel's hands—now cold like ice—and she would be free of him. He would die and she would need to care no longer.

But I do care.

She had no more reason than that. If she did not care, then she was as bad as all the rest with nothing to commend her. Her life would have no meaning.

She opened her mouth to speak but found it so dry she could say nothing. The fibres of gold dimmed towards the blackness that threatened to engulf them.

Something heavy came down on her shoulder.

And with it, a flood of golden brightness that she feared would blind her. The light flowed into her head and down her body, ran along her arms and out.

Yenteel jerked and his hands almost pulled away from hers but she held on. The pattern that had almost faded from view exploded into life. The threads were alive once more, moving and weaving. If she could have shut her mind's eye she would have done it willingly as the power flowed through her and into Yenteel.

It took mere moments, but seemed like eternity. The pattern was complete. Its image vanished from her mind. She slipped her hands from Yenteel's but the weight on her shoulder remained.

Sheesha grumbled in her ear. She turned and saw one side of his massive jaw resting on her shoulder. His mouth was easily big enough to swallow her entire head, while his teeth, barely a hands-breadth from her eyes, were the length of her fingers. The eye on this side was looking directly at her.

"Thank you," she said quietly.

In an effortless motion, Sheesha lifted his head and grumbled again as he stretched his wings.

"Ow! Get off, idiot."

In the silver light of Lostimal she saw Daybian on his hands and knees with Sheesha's wing directly over him. Whether he had ducked to avoid it or been knocked over she had no idea, but it looked comical.

Then she yawned and a wave of fatigue swept through her. She felt as if she had run a thousand leagues. The dark world around her went fuzzy. She rubbed her eyes, but it didn't help. Then she fell back into the grass and forgot about everything.

The sun was above the trees when she woke. There was a blanket over her and saddlebags under her head. She felt comfortable and relaxed. When she realised the headache she expected wasn't there, she settled back into the saddle bags.

Then she remembered why she expected a headache.

The blanket flew off her and she stood up. Sheesha and Looesa were gone again. Jintan and Shingul were splashing in the pool. Beyond them she could see two men; one of them was Daybian, the other was dark and thin. They appeared to be leaning over the body of the man they had pulled from the water.

Where was Gally?

She turned again. He was beside the smouldering fire, putting down fresh branches.

Everything was calm.

Yenteel? She realised that he was not lying beside her, and immediately after, that he was the gaunt fellow with Daybian.

Everyone was up except her. She sat down. The healing must have been successful. She glanced back at the two. Yenteel was using a branch as a walking stick and his injured arm was still in a sling. Well, they had not attempted to fix that.

She considered what had happened. Romain had never mentioned that the *zirichasa* were strong with magic. She was certain he could not have known. They never exhibited anything like that. They did not have fire-tubes like the *tekrasa*; they did not communicate mind-to-mind like wolves—she had to admit defeat at that point, as her examples ran out. She had no idea what other animals might have magic.

Though she had heard a lot of tales, like monstrous *nachasa* the size of mountains. But she had always dismissed those as imaginative stories to scare young children.

But there was nothing told about the *ziri*. Even when she had spoken to other keepers at the races, they boasted about their charges. Of course, she had done it too. But never had any one of them hinted that *zirichasa* might be capable of some magic or other.

Nobody knew.

Nobody except her. And what did she even know? That Sheesha had touched her and given her energy that she could then pass on to Yenteel so that he could complete his patterning? It was vague, and perhaps she had imagined it. It might have been that the power came from her and she had unleashed it by accident.

Yes. If anybody asked that's what she would say. If she told the truth, who knew what terrible things would happen to the *ziri*? People would try to use them for patternings. They would be cut up and sold in markets as cures for this and that.

She shook her head.

Yenteel had said she was a good liar. So that's what she would do.

She needed to relieve herself but decided her hunger needed

assuaging first. There was still some cold cooked meat from yesterday which she helped herself to. She felt guilty for a moment, as if she were stealing it because she had not asked anyone. Then she remembered that the only person she needed to ask was herself—or possibly Sheesha, since he'd caught it. However, he wasn't here and she did not think he would begrudge her a meal.

After taking a handful of the meat, she headed across to the other side of the stream to see what they were discussing.

Daybian was holding the coat she had rescued. He and Yenteel had moved away from the body, which had been gnawed down to the bone. The air above it was filled with flies.

"We shall be heading west," said Daybian as she approached.

"I'm sorry?"

Daybian pointed. "We'll go west."

She gritted her teeth. "I see."

Yenteel looked a dozen years older than he had before.

"I must thank you for your help, Kantees." His voice was also weak but better than it had been.

"I am always pleased to be able to help someone who needs it," she said. "But next time I shall be more careful with patterners. I believe you almost killed me as well as yourself."

"But you had enough strength."

"Barely." *If not for Sheesha, we would both be carrion.*

"In that case my gratitude is redoubled." He tried for a sweeping bow but stumbled in the process and caught himself with the stick only at the last moment.

"Why do you think we should go west?" she said to Yenteel, ignoring Daybian.

"I recognise the coat," said Daybian.

"I asked Yenteel."

"But I knew the answer."

Kantees closed her eyes. Perhaps she was more tired than she thought. One thing was certain, her temper was not good. But, damn it, Daybian had no right.

Why wasn't she saying this out loud? She turned to Daybian.

"You are not in charge of this ..." Words failed her.

"What?"

She gestured to Yenteel and then back to where Gally worked on the fire. "Us."

"I do not have to remind you, Kantees, that my family owns—"

"*Be careful what you say right now,*" she hissed. "*Or you just might be walking back to your family.*"

"—the *ziri*. My family owns the *zirichasa*."

"I'm borrowing them."

"You've stolen them."

"Yes," she said. "That's right, I have stolen them so they are not yours any longer. They're mine."

"Perhaps we could discuss this later?" said Yenteel.

Just then Shingul and Jintan let out the booming calls that heralded the return of the hunting pair. Daybian turned in surprise to see them stretching their necks up, mouths open to amplify the call.

"Are they all right?" said Daybian. "Are they ill?"

Kantees found her anger evaporating. At least Daybian was honest in his regard of the *ziri* and he was genuinely concerned.

"Did they make that noise yesterday?" said Yenteel. "I seem to recall it from a dream."

"It means Sheesha and Looesa are on their way back," she said. "I didn't know why either, when they did that yesterday." She scanned the skies and saw the dots.

She pointed. "There."

17

Despite Kantees' concerns about further delay, she didn't argue about staying another night so Yenteel could gain more strength. Besides, it was late in the day and they wouldn't be able to fly for long.

The blanket that had covered her belonged to Daybian and, while the rest of them slept with the *ziri*—not completely comfortable but warm—he chose not to.

Kantees was tired, but even snuggled under Sheesha's feathers and warmed against his body, she had trouble going to sleep.

Everything suddenly felt overwhelming. The world stretched into forever. Her crimes hung round her neck like a millstone. The power of the *zirichasa* was too important. And the *tekrak* had been too big. And where there was one, there would be more. And with them, the people who had taken Jelamie.

Why had they taken him? He was just an annoying child. He wasn't the heir, merely the spare in case something happened to Daybian.

And Daybian was here, in danger of ending the line of Jakalain by getting himself killed in an attempt to rescue his brother who might already be dead. She did not ask for the responsibility of watching over him. He would probably say that he did not require her to do so.

What am I doing? she asked herself again, who knew how many times in the last few days, and she still didn't have a good answer. In the end, all she could think of was that she was trying to do the right thing. But what right did she have to decide what that was?

She had a painful awakening when Sheesha decided it was time to get up. He rolled onto his rear legs and simply stood. Somehow the rolling motion had invaded her dream as a fall from a great height and she only really woke when she hit the ground. Even then, for a moment, she was not entirely sure what was real and what was not.

Sheesha stretched his wings and shook them out so the feathers aligned properly. He bent his neck backwards and his lower back upwards, all the way from the tip of his nose to the tip of his tail, so he was shaped like a cup. He grunted, relaxed, and brought his head round to look Kantees straight in the face. Every time he did this, for this was not the first, was comical as he focused his wide-spread eyes on her. He looked cross-eyed.

And his breath smelled awful.

"Yes," she said. "We're going."

The rest of the camp was not up but Sheesha prodded the other *ziri*. Jintan snapped at him, then ducked his head when Sheesha rumbled ominously. Looesa tipped Gally onto the grass, but Yenteel was spared such abuse. Once again, Shingul had been lying over him to keep him warm instead of having him lie on her.

Kantees went off to the edge of the wood to do the necessary and then headed up to wash where the stream entered the pool. The sun was not high; they would be able to get a good distance today.

Daybian appeared beside her. He had stripped off his shirt to reveal his pasty white skin. If he thought it would make him more attractive to her, he was sadly mistaken. In truth, it had the opposite effect. She stood up as he bent down to splash the water on his face.

"What's west?" she said.

"What do you mean?"

"Why should we go west? You seemed very sure of yourself."

"That fellow"—he waved his hand in the direction of the corpse still lying out on the grass across the stream—"comes from Kurvin Port."

"How do you know?"

"The design on the coat. He's a Hamalain and, from his age, he'll almost certainly be one of the family. They are very rich and influential in the Conclave. I've met Deenya, the sister, and seen Trimiente, nasty piece of work. This is probably Lorima."

"Well, he was one of the raiders."

"Yes." Daybian stood up and looked at her. "This is dangerous."

She couldn't believe it. Was he serious in thinking she didn't know what situation they were in? "Is it that you think all women are stupid, Daybian? Or just slave women?"

He looked hurt. "I honestly do not understand you, Kantees."

"That, Daybian," she said, "is the first intelligent thing to come out of your mouth."

She realised she was just getting angry again, which meant she was getting off the subject. She took a deep breath and calmed herself down.

"I know this is dangerous, Daybian, even if we find Jelamie. I'm still under a sentence of death."

"Why don't you just run away to the mountains, then?"

"Because I'm responsible," she said. "But afterwards, yes, I might just do that."

"Not everything is your responsibility. You're a slave. Your responsibility ends with the job you do."

She closed her eyes again to help suppress the violence that wanted to erupt from her. He really did not understand. To hear him you would think that being a slave was a lovely life, no need to worry about anything. Except being beaten, whipped, raped, or killed at the whim of your master because you were nothing more than a possession. Like a cheap ceramic cup. If you fell and broke into a thousand pieces it might be a shame in the moment, but it did not matter in the long run. Another could always be bought.

"You are such an idiot, Daybian," she said quietly. "You think you know so much."

They returned to the camp and found Gally saddling the *ziri* even though Kantees had not told him to. The meat from two days ago had been eaten but there was fresh from the previous day's kills. She and Daybian ate in silence.

Sheesha and Looesa were good hunters, and considerate enough to bring food back. That surprised her. As far as she knew Sheesha had been bred in captivity and always had been fed dead animals. He had never needed to catch his own. She did not know about Looesa, but he was so tame she could not imagine he had ever had to hunt.

Yet here they were, experts. And the others knew how to call to them—in ways they had never used at the castle.

Perhaps it had something to do with their magic. It didn't matter —she was not going to discuss it with anyone.

Yenteel was stronger and his skin looked healthier than it had at any time in the last couple of days. He would probably want to perform the healer patterning on his arm again, but for now he seemed happy enough with it in the sling.

"Have you given any thought to how we will enter Kurvin Port?" he said.

"You know about Kurvin Port," said Kantees.

"That's where the Hamalain have their dominion."

"I haven't thought about it," said Kantees. "Since I have only just been told. Obviously we cannot fly in but neither can we leave the *ziri* on their own."

"Gally can look after them," said Gally.

She smiled at him. "I know, Gally, and I trust you. But it's not out of concern for the *ziri*, it's about people who might find them."

"Gally doesn't like people." He frowned.

"I know something of the place," said Yenteel. "The mountains come almost down to the sea all around and Kurvin Port itself is in a wide bay with cliffs around it. There are farms on the slopes that supply it."

"That's nice."

"But the cliffs run for leagues along the coast on that side with hundreds of small bays, and many of those have fishing villages."

"Fishing villages may not be as bad as Kurvin Port," she said. "But we still can't fly into them."

"I can," said Daybian.

"But we can't."

As if attempting to forestall another argument, Yenteel cut in. "The cliffs have caves. We just need to find a bay that doesn't have a village, but does have a cave, that's close to Kurvin Port. The *zirichasa* can remain there with Gally while we go into the town."

"I am not clear on our plan when we've arrived," said Kantees. "Just because we know what family the man came from, how does that get us any closer to finding Jelamie?"

"I think," said Yenteel, "we will have to see what happens."

"We can enter the town with you two as my servants," said Daybian. "I can talk to the Hamalain as an equal. I'll report the death of this brother and then we can find out what he was doing raiding the Jakalain."

Kantees watched in amusement as even Daybian realised that wasn't going to work. She looked at the sun crossing the sky.

"That's enough of a plan," she said, "until we can find out more."

There was a short discussion when Daybian still thought he was going to ride Sheesha. But it was the *ziri* himself who settled that by walking up and standing behind Kantees. She could not resist a grin at Daybian's expense.

That Shingul would carry Yenteel was a foregone conclusion, as she seemed to have adopted him. Gally already had the reins of Looesa. Even Daybian did not have the heart to deliberately upset the lad. So he rode old Jintan again.

"He's a remarkably strong *zirichak* for his age," said Daybian as he mounted and gave Jintan's neck an affectionate thump.

Kantees double-checked Yenteel's saddle buckles because he had been almost unconscious the previous time he had flown and she was not sure how he might react now he was truly awake.

"There is no need to mother me, Kantees," he said for her ears only.

"How would you know?" she said. "You have no experience of *ziri*, you do not know what is right or wrong. You are in no position to judge."

Once more, he had no answer but gave her a nod in acknowledgement.

Whether it was something the *ziri* did without thinking she did not know, but they had arranged themselves on the ground in a diamond shape. Sheesha was at the head, Looesa and Shingul ranged to the left and right behind, and Jintan waited in the rear.

She gave Sheesha a little kick. He spread his powerful wings and stroked them downward. He lifted effortlessly. Wingbeat after wingbeat pushed them upward and she thrilled once more at the sensation as the ground dropped away.

Looking behind she saw the others in exactly the same formation as they had been on the ground. She had noticed it before but with the new revelations about the creatures, she saw it with new eyes. The only thing that did not match were their wingbeats.

She let Sheesha choose their flying height once she had pointed him in the right direction—or the best approximation of 'the right direction' she could manage. She still did not know how big Esternes was and the trouble with using a patterner's path—direct travel from ley-circle to ley-circle—was that it gave no indication of the true distance.

In the past, when they had gone to the races, they had always gone by the path. The patterners would chant and inscribe their patterns on the ground to create an invisible gate, you walked into the gate and through the World's Pattern until you reached the gate at the end. The strangest thing about the journey was that you never knew how long it would take.

Even the journey from her old master to Jakalain had been by ley-circle. Her old master had maps but he kept them locked up because they were so valuable.

So, the matter of the size of Esternes was important. How long would it take for a *ziri* to cross it?

The wood where they had camped was swiftly lost to view. The ground appeared flat but it was an undulating surface cut by streams and rivers that flowed from the mountains. Yenteel had said the mountains went to the edge of the sea, so if they followed the mountains they would also reach the sea. Then they could follow the cliffs.

Or they could ask someone.

Villages, sometimes fewer than a dozen buildings grouped together, dotted the landscape. Now that they were travelling in daylight she could see that each village was surrounded by a high fence—which also enclosed areas for animals. Beyond the walls, in almost every case, were herds of *fenichasa* with men, sometimes boys, guarding them.

Just as she looked down, the herdsmen and the people in the villages looked up at the four *ziri* passing across the sky. She wondered what those people thought. Did they see the riders? They must. Sheesha was not flying very high and it was easy enough to see the people down there, so Kantees, Gally, Yenteel, and Daybian must be clearly visible.

Not that it mattered. It would be days before any of these people could pass on a message to someone who mattered even if they wanted to.

Then there was forest.

Almost as if there was a line across the land. Nothing lay below them but trees, and packed so close together only the tops were visible. The undulating green was cut by the occasional wide river. Birds and other flying creatures populated the upper reaches of the trees but what lay below she had no idea.

The sun told her it was getting towards midday. The *ziri* had been flying all that time and must be getting tired. But they were still over the forest, which now stretched from horizon to horizon in all direc-tions except to the north, where the mountains grew out of the green.

She began to look in earnest for a place to land.

None of the rivers seemed to have any islands and she was concerned about what nasty things might live in their waters. Her time with the scholar had educated her enough that she knew no place in the world was free of creatures that would like to eat you.

She would have preferred an open hilltop, so they could at least see when an enemy was approaching, but the trees covered everything.

"Hey!"

It was Yenteel. She turned and saw him pointing off towards the mountains. She peered in that direction and saw what looked like a gap in the trees. He must have been thinking the same thing.

She made Sheesha wheel that way, confident the others would follow. It was a gap, large and circular. Suddenly this did not look like a good idea. As they closed in on it, she could see the trees growing around its edge were twisted and discoloured. The ground itself was devoid of any life. Not a single plant or animal that she could see.

"Ley-circle!" she shouted back and shook her head. "Not safe."

"No feeding!"

She frowned. How could he know that? The feeding at Jakalain had been barely three days ago and it was unlikely there would be another conjunction so close. But she knew from her time at her first master's house that it was more complicated than that; sometimes feedings did happen within a day of each other, though never in the same place. Questions about feedings were frequent and Kevrey would turn most of them away. It was dangerous territory.

She made the decision and put Sheesha into a descent towards the circle. Not the middle, but not too close to the edge. Who knew what pattern-corrupted abominations might be lurking among the distorted trees?

18

The fact that Sheesha and the other *ziri* did not seem concerned at landing in the ley-circle gave Kantees some confidence. Perhaps magical creatures would be able to sense trouble.

The surface of the circle was damp soil. It must have rained recently. The Taymalin always put stone down in their circles—preferably the hardest stone they could find, because it resisted the warping in all but the biggest circles. But this one must be unknown to the Taymalin, and perhaps anyone else. She and her companions might have been the first people ever to set foot here.

If anything went wrong they might also be the last. A part of her mind suggested that perhaps they were not the first and the bones of the others were here too, perhaps just beneath the surface. Or blasted to dust by the power of a feeding.

As soon as Looesa had landed, Gally set about removing his saddle and other tack. She almost stopped him but the *ziri* needed to eat and they could not hunt while saddled. So she followed suit with Sheesha while keeping an eye on Yenteel, who was slowly unbuckling himself.

Instead of removing Jintan's saddle, Daybian drew his short sword and prowled around them as if he was looking for trouble. In this she neither blamed him nor wanted him to stop. This was an unsettling place.

It was unnerving to know that, every once in a while, a pillar of white light would descend from the heavens into this space and everything within it would be consumed. No one truly knew what happened. Anything too close was changed and twisted. Yet it was not a malignant force. This was the power of the healers and the patterners, but in such quantity that the patterns of everything within its reach were changed. Or died.

As soon as they were free, Sheesha, Jintan, and Looesa leapt into the air. The closeness of the trees meant they were soon out of sight.

Kantees went to where Yenteel stood, leaning against Shingul's body.

"Do you know where we are?" she said.

He shook his head. "Not precisely. However, this is most likely the Talamyrth, the forest that covers Esternes to the west and south. It would make sense."

"And this ley-circle?"

"I don't know. There are many circles that are not used by people and this one is inaccessible."

"A patterner could make a path to it."

"Only if he knew what he was looking for."

She sighed. "I don't like it." Then she looked at the twisted wall of trees. "And I'm scared of what's out there."

"That is wise," he said.

"Not very encouraging."

"It wasn't meant to be. Only a fool would not be afraid. Even our friend Daybian is not that much of a fool."

Daybian looked up as he heard his name. Kantees scowled at him and he looked away, scanning the trees again.

"What if there's a feeding?"

"There won't be."

"How can you say that?"

Yenteel reached into his bag, glanced once in Daybian's direction, then pulled out a circular device. It had wheels within wheels. He turned it, lining up sections.

"You can't have that," Kantees hissed.

It was Yenteel's turn to look surprised. "You know what it is?"

"I know owning it means death."

"Well, we've already committed enough crimes to be hanged six times over," said Yenteel. "And this tells me there isn't another feeding for several days. Chances are the next one will not be in our lands at all."

"When you say *our* lands, do you mean the Taymalin or the Kadralin?"

"There is not much difference, since the Taymalin occupy all the Kadralin lands."

Kantees looked up towards the mountains. "But not there."

Yenteel turned and followed her gaze, then shook his head. "There is nothing there, Kantees. The centre of Esternes is not habitable by the likes of us. Only the giant *sikechasa* live there, and the prey they feed on."

"I heard our people are free there."

"Tales made to give us hope. More likely you would find the *Slissac* alive and well and crawling about in their holes."

"You have no hope, then?"

"I don't believe in children's stories, Kantees. I believe in what I can sense." For a moment he hesitated. She could see the decision being made on his face, until he said, more quietly, "And I believe in you."

A wave of fear shot through her and she turned away. "I don't want to know."

"Kantees …" He put his hand on her shoulder.

She shrugged it off, took a step away and turned on him. "Leave me alone."

The sudden movement and her words attracted Daybian's attention and she looked skyward as he strode over.

"What's wrong, Kantees? Does this slave need putting in his place?"

"Shut up. This has nothing to do with you."

She glared at them both. Yenteel with a pleading look on his face, and Daybian both angry and confused. Then she saw Gally looking over.

"Just leave me alone," she said. "This is hard enough without you two confusing things. You." She looked at Yenteel. "I don't want to know why you were at Jakalain and I am certainly not interested in your master's interpretation of the World's Pattern. And you." This time she addressed Daybian. "Stop trying to protect me. You don't own me and I do not want your help."

She turned away and walked a few paces but it took her closer to the maze of trees and she was forced to stop. There was nowhere she could go to be out of their sight. If only Sheesha would return. She could climb into his saddle and leave them behind.

Except she wouldn't. She couldn't.

The other *ziri* would follow Sheesha and she would not abandon these people. Especially not Gally.

So instead she stared into the darkness beyond the exposed trees. Not that they looked much like trees. Their trunks and branches were split with holes through them and, instead of simply growing up to where their leaves could catch the sunlight, they grew in every direction. She followed one branch from where it split off a trunk to where it fed into another one, as if it was one branch for two trees.

Perhaps this was not a bad thing. It meant the confused mass made a barrier against anything large. But then her experience with the *chakisa*-like creatures had shown her that even small could be dangerous in sufficient numbers.

Her skin crawled at the thought of what might be lurking out there. And as she stared, a shadow moved in the dark beyond. A limb of something blocked out a stray light that had managed to pierce the trees, and then revealed it again.

She shuddered.

She did not dare turn her back and, even though she felt a fool, she took steps backwards, keeping her eyes on the spot where she had seen the movement.

We can't stay here overnight. Her shadow was lengthening but she knew without having to check the sky that they still had a good amount of light left.

Something touched her shoulder.

She jumped.

"Sorry," said Yenteel. "You seemed worried."

"Nearly jumped out of my skin, you idiot. You could have just said something."

"The last time I said something you jumped down my throat."

"There's something moving in the dark," she said.

"The place is alive."

"What do you mean?"

"I simply mean this is a forest and there are living things out there. It can't be considered a surprise that there would be things moving in the dark. It doesn't mean they are dangerous to us."

"Something in the forest will be able to kill us."

"That's always true, Kantees. The world is not safe."

"Do you know how much cooked meat we have left?"

"Is that my job? Am I the keeper of the provisions?"

She sighed. "Can you just tell me whether you know or not?"

"I don't."

"Fine."

Kantees turned away from the forest and headed for the pile of belongings. She noted that Gally had already helped himself to a strip of meat and was chewing it. She checked the rest. It was enough for another day, more if they were careful. Daybian might not appreciate short rations but the rest of them would not complain.

Yenteel had spent some time looking into the trees where she had indicated but then joined her. Daybian appeared to have given up patrolling and sat down with his back against Shingul, who did not seem to mind.

"We're moving on as soon as Sheesha and Looesa get back," she said without preamble.

"We should rest them," said Daybian.

"It's not safe here."

"As safe as anywhere else, Kantees," said Yenteel. "We can't know that we'll find anywhere else to set down before dark."

"There is no wood for a fire," she said. "And no way to fetch any through the trees. They are all grown together, with only enough space for a *chakik*. Even if we dared go into that wood, which I do not."

That stopped them. She knew she was being driven by her fear but she had to make them see that they could not stay here.

"I'm sure I could break off some branches," said Daybian.

"Be my guest," she said. "We have no tools so you would have to climb into that. Whatever it is that's there will be able to grab you, or bite you, or sting you, or just eat you whole."

"I am not afraid, Kantees," said Daybian.

"That's because you're too stupid to have an imagination!" she said, and instantly wished she hadn't when the look of hurt crossed his face.

"You think I am *stupid?*"

"No, I—"

"You think I'm stupid," he said. "Now I understand. That's why you wouldn't lie with me."

"*What?* You're still talking about that?" She took a deep breath. "I am sorry I called you stupid. I was angry. I have already told you why I will not lie with you, but if you insist I'll say it again. I am not interested in you. You may have been my master but that still doesn't mean I would wish you to have your way with me. But don't take it personally, it's not you. I don't want anybody."

Yenteel and Gally were staring at her. She immediately felt herself flushing with embarrassment. How had they got onto this subject? Oh yes, Daybian and his inability to think with anything except his loins.

"When Sheesha, Looesa and Jintan get back we will give the *ziri* enough time to eat and digest their food. Then we are leaving."

"And if it's dark by then?" said Yenteel.

"We'll either be dead or we'll be leaving. And that's final."

The *zirichasa* did not seem to mind flying at night so there was no reason they should not do it again. Sheesha would understand.

There was nothing to be done while they waited. They were hedged in by the trees and the ground was bare and uninteresting. Only the clouds above their heads had any degree of variety, so Kantees lay down with her head on a saddle and stared up at the slow-moving shapes against the blue sky.

It was hot but there was no shade. Or rather the only shade that existed—cast by Shingul's body—had been taken by Daybian and then Yenteel. She did not begrudge the injured man since he needed his rest. But she was not happy with Daybian. He did it as if it was his birthright, his privilege. In other circumstances, back at Jakalain, he would be right, but not now and not here.

She dozed off to be woken with a start by Shingul booming into the sky.

The sun had moved and was low in the sky. Had they had trouble finding food? She hoped they had not exhausted themselves. They dropped three animals, two of which were four-legged like the ones they had caught before. The third, carried by Sheesha, was another winged creature, almost half his size. This one had a beak, so was not a *ziri* but just a large bird. It might have good meat. But they couldn't do anything with it apart from cut it up.

Sheesha strutted around after he landed. Kantees smiled. She had seen him do that before when he had almost won a race. The other racing *ziri* did it too. He must be proud of himself. Then she saw the blood on his side.

She ran over to him and pushed the feathers out of the way. A gash in his side was leaking blood. She felt around the wound and dug her fingers into his muscle. The cut wasn't too deep and did not seem to have affected his ability to fly but he was limping a little.

"You idiot," she said to him. "You had to take something that wanted to fight back. Next time just grab a fledgling. Or a shellfish—you love those." All *ziri* did, drove them wild, although they didn't get them much in Jakalain.

She looked at the sun and back at the wound. And felt her plans coming crashing down.

"Yenteel, can you heal this?"

He came over and examined the damage, and then Sheesha. "We haven't got anything big enough to mark the pattern."

"We can't stay here."

"Then you must make Sheesha fly," he said and then looked at the other *ziri*. Looesa and Jintan were already curled up while Shingul tore chunks out of one of the carcasses. "But while I may not be as experienced as you with *zirichasa*, they look tired."

Mother's milk. He was right, of course. She just didn't want to admit it.

"I can try to put up a ward," he said. "But it would have to be big and I don't know if I have the strength to activate it."

"I can help," she said.

He nodded but still seemed unsure.

"How much power does it need?"

"It would need to be big enough to enclose everyone," he said, "and last all through the night."

"I thought ley-circles were the sources of power," she said and he stared at her.

"They are."

"We're standing in a big one."

"Yes," he said and looked down then grinned. "We are."

"What do you need?"

"I have to be able to draw an exact pattern in a circle."

"Where do you need to draw it?"

"In the ground."

Kantees looked up. "Daybian, lend Yenteel your sword."

"I will not. You called me stupid."

"Stop behaving like a child. He needs to be able to create a pattern that will protect us through the night."

"So now I'm a child?"

"*Kisharuk's curse!* Just give him your milk-sucking sword!"

She stalked off to where Gally sat staring at the trees.

"Bad things in trees, Kantees."

"I know, Gally. Yenteel needs your help to draw a big circle so he can make a pattern that will protect us."

"You said we fly away," he said.

"I did say that, but Sheesha got into a fight and he has a nasty scratch. So we have to stay."

"Gally will help."

"Thank you, Gally. Be quick."

Kantees did not know how long it would take to make the circle but she was sure that whatever was in the trees would come out the moment the clearing was as dark as it was in the forest. Perhaps sooner.

19

The sun was brushing the top of the trees on the west side of the circle. And Yenteel was busy working with the sword, scratching patterns into the dry soil.

She wondered how accurate he needed to be. He had spent several minutes trying to find the centre of the ley-circle itself, though he had done that by eye. The point he chose looked right to her though it may have been off a little, and there he made a hole in the ground to mark the place. Not only did nothing live in the ley-circle, there were no stones. As if everything had been pulverised to dust.

Meanwhile Kantees had untied one set of reins to use in drawing the pattern. Gally held one end in the hole while Yenteel stretched it taut and used the sword to mark the first circle. Then they did it again but with the reins shortened by the length of his forearm. The next stage was to mark off twelve equal segments between the two circles, which was a matter of trial and error.

After that it was just Yenteel making patterns, using the sword as a stylus, in each of the segments. Although he was working with large symbols it seemed to take forever as the sun descended.

She tried to pretend it was her imagination when she saw movement in the trees on the west side, in the deepest shade. But Gally noticed and pointed. Kantees looked at Daybian, who was staring in the same direction. Then he glanced at Yenteel with his sword, obviously wishing he had it instead.

Only the *ziri* seemed unconcerned because the three who had gone hunting were now asleep, but Shingul did seem to be keeping an eye on the movement. Perhaps they were being cautious too. Creatures of their size did not have many enemies but Kantees would be upset if they chose to fly away in the event of an attack.

She hoped it wouldn't come to that.

And what would happen if they were inside the protection but Sheesha decided he had been provoked and wanted to fight again? In some ways he seemed to be a typical male, though she liked him a good deal more than Daybian, and even Yenteel.

She was aware it was pointless worrying over things she could not control. But knowing that did not help at all.

By the time Yenteel was on the penultimate segment, the sun's light was only brushing the tops of the trees. The movement in the trees was constant, though she could not see what was there. It was as if the shadows themselves had come alive.

If they were going to trust the pattern they needed to get inside it now.

"Daybian, fetch your sleeping blanket." He opened his mouth to speak. "Don't argue, please, just do it. Gally, collect all the tack together. We need to get it into the pattern."

While that was happening, she went to Sheesha and gently woke him by repeating his name into his ear. Just like any person, Sheesha did not like to be woken suddenly. That had been a painful lesson to learn and she rubbed her cheek unconsciously.

The big *ziri* woke the other two. There was a flurry of shadows and a skittering noise she had not heard before. Clearly the sight of four big *zirichasa* wide awake was upsetting to their observers. Sheesha gave a low growl in the direction of the trees.

"Lay the blanket over the lines in the last segment," she said to Daybian. "Then we need to move everything inside. Try not to step on the lines."

She knew they should have done that earlier but she didn't want to crowd Yenteel. There wasn't going to be a great deal of space with four people, four *ziri*, and their gear.

The first attempt at getting Sheesha into the pattern was a disaster. In the air he was perfection, but on land he was clumsy and immediately dragged the blanket across the ground, obliterating the markings.

Kantees went numb staring at the gap. Having been about to start on that last segment, Yenteel stopped and stared at the damage. Then up at Kantees.

"I can still see the lines," he said, though his voice was strained.

"Gally! Get the tack back on the *ziri*. Just enough to fly them. Daybian, you keep moving everything else into the pattern."

She pulled Sheesha across to the saddle and threw it on his back.

The shadows were moaning.

As she fastened and tightened the buckles round his body, Sheesha growled and hissed at the shapes in the dark. She did not stop to see if it had any effect but had to yank his head down to get the bridle in place.

"I've finished," called Daybian.

"Fly Sheesha into the pattern. Hurry."

Daybian ran over to her and grabbed the reins. He pulled himself up.

"Don't touch the lines," she said.

He held her gaze for a moment and nodded.

The blast from Sheesha's wings blew her off balance and for a terrified moment she thought it might have scrubbed the pattern, but it looked undamaged. Yenteel was working on the final segment, having scratched the marks afresh through the places where they had been obliterated.

Gally had Jintan ready.

She wasn't sure what to do. Gally was no rider. He just sat on the *ziri*'s back and let it follow the rest.

"Do Looesa," she said and hurried to Shingul just as Daybian brought Sheesha down lightly into the pattern. Kantees shook her head. How could they all fit into the space? Daybian was off in a trice and got Sheesha to back up to the edge of the markings, then lie down with his tail circled around him.

Kantees made the mistake of looking into the shadows. As the sun went down her eyes had adjusted and now she could see what watched them. They looked like men. If men were covered in hair. And they were getting into the ley-circle by climbing over the wall of interconnected trees. Some of them carried clubs and they were heading slowly towards her and the pattern.

She tore her eyes away from the scene and back to the job in hand.

There isn't enough time.

"Kantees, I'm ready!" shouted Yenteel just as Daybian leapt out of the pattern and ran for Jintan. Gally was tightening the reins on Looesa, but froze as he saw the figures coming slowly towards them. She heard him cry in fear. By then, Daybian was into the saddle and kicking the old *zirichak* into the air.

"Gally! Go to Yenteel. Now!" She put everything she had into the command. He looked at her. She pointed forcefully.

"But Kantees…"

"Go!" He went, at a run.

Kantees stared. There was no time to get Shingul's tack buckled on.

"Kantees!" shouted Daybian from above. "Leave them. They can fly."

But where would they go? They needed to rest somewhere safe. Assuming Yenteel could get his pattern to work. She saw Jintan coming down in the middle of it. She had to admit Daybian was an excellent rider, despite all his other—many—faults.

"Yenteel, do it." She forced her voice to calm. "Come on, Shingul."

Kantees sprinted across to Looesa and jumped into the saddle. No time to buckle in. The figures were close and the noise of their moans, which seemed to be resolving into some sort of chant, increased.

Looesa snapped at them. In answer, one of them swung a club. The *ziri* evaded it easily, but there were more coming.

"Up, Looesa! Come on, Shingul!"

Looesa stretched his neck upwards; his wings beat hard and he lifted into the air in spurts that drove them from the ground. She clung to the reins. Gally had done his job right and they were firm. She glanced back. Shingul had lifted from the ground. A club buzzed past her head.

She almost cried out in anger and frustration. Damn these things! Why weren't they as stupid as … Daybian. A blue glow flooded the ley-circle. The inscribed pattern lit up. She prayed that either it did not reach as high as her, or that Yenteel's conjuration was not yet complete.

With a movement of the reins she guided Looesa over the glowing light and tried to make him drop vertically. There was little enough room below; *ziri* did not land straight down unless there was no space. As far as Looesa could see he had plenty of room despite the creatures closing in on all sides. He flew beyond the confines of the pattern. She pulled him round.

They liked to gain height using spirals, so why not land the same way? It would have to be a very tight spiral.

She pulled the right rein hard in and leaned her weight over to the right, unbalancing Looesa. He turned into it but she kept it tight and he descended, almost turning on his right wingtip. Kantees hoped Shingul was following.

Below her Yenteel was kneeling on the unmarked dirt just inside the inner circle of the pattern, with his hands palms-down by the final segment he had drawn. She could not imagine how much pain his injured arm must be in. Sheesha and Jintan were standing and snapping aggressively at the incoming figures while Daybian was being jerked between both their reins, one in each hand, as he kept them from leaving the pattern.

The glow intensified suddenly and a wall of blue erupted around them. Looesa's wing caught on it. He lost all forward motion and fell the remaining distance to crash down in front of Sheesha's head. Another pile of feathers landed directly on top of Daybian.

All noise from outside ceased but there were plenty of angry squawks and shouts from the animals and humans inside. Kantees slipped off Looesa's back onto the hard earth facing the wall of blue light. She could see through it, as if it were blue glass, but it did not distort what was beyond.

The creatures had stopped a short distance away.

Worried, she got to her feet and went across to where Yenteel knelt. She went down beside him. There was a look of concentration on his face.

"It's working, Yenteel."

He said nothing.

"Will it hold?"

Again he said nothing, almost as if he did not hear her. She reached out and put her hand on his bare forearm. Instantly she felt her essence draining, just as it had done before when he had healed himself.

They could not survive the night if he had to keep it going. Surely he had said that it would use the power from the ley-circle? But as she thought about it, he had not said that. Did he expect her to be able to provide magic?

She called out to Sheesha and almost at the same moment his head came down beside her. She put her other hand on his neck and felt his power. So much of it. Like a bottomless well. And she was the conduit. It flowed through her into Yenteel.

The look of desperation on Yenteel's face relaxed and the blue light increased in strength. For a moment she felt a greater power even than Sheesha. Then Yenteel pulled his hands from the wall of blue.

She gasped in fear that it would collapse. But it stayed.

And then Sheesha was just Sheesha. She let go of Yenteel's arm and he put his other back in its sling. The creatures beyond the wall did not seem to want to come too close. Perhaps there was just too much light for them here.

She reached out and touched the blue wall. It was neither hot nor cold and she could not see what she was pressing her finger against. The surface was unyielding but perfectly smooth.

"We did it," she said and looked round. They were all here, all the people and all the *ziri*. "Thank you, Yenteel."

He grinned as he touched the wall himself and ran his fingers from side to side across its surface.

"I've never done one this big," he said as if he was in awe. "I wasn't even sure it would draw magic from the ley-circle itself."

"You knew what to do," she said. "If it wasn't for you, we would be dead."

"And me," said Daybian.

"And Gally," said Gally.

Sheesha grunted.

20

When dawn crawled into the sky the creatures seem to melt away with it. Although it was easy to see them crawling across the upper branches of the trees and out into the darkness beyond.

The *ziri* had slept—and snored—just as Gally, Yenteel, and Daybian had.

But Kantees only dozed. She would drift off and then come awake as the thought of the horde beyond the insubstantial wall crept into her dreams. As the night wore on it became hot and stuffy in their protected space, as if the air itself were turning stale. That stopped her sleeping too. There had been a time when she had been locked in a box with no air. It was not something she recalled with any clarity but it came into her nightmares.

The coming of daylight was a relief even if she felt so tired she could drop off again. And the air was such she hardly felt as if she could breathe.

The ward itself seemed as strong as ever and it went up until it blurred into the sky. If she had not got Looesa and Shingul inside it when she did, they would have been trapped outside, and forced to find somewhere to spend the night in that forest.

She wondered about the manlike things. Were they people who

had been distorted by the power of the feeding? She was curious but it was a mystery she was happy to leave unsolved.

One of the *ziri* shat and the stench filled the space.

"Yenteel," she said, shaking him. "Do you know how to stop it? We need to get out, we need fresh air."

It took longer than she expected for him to wake up. At first, he did not seem to remember where he was.

Finally she got him to the wall.

"Do what you have to do," she said. Behind her the *ziri* were waking and stretching their necks so their heads were up high. That seemed to rouse them. They dipped their heads but every now and then would stretch up to breathe.

Yenteel had his hands against the wall but nothing was happening.

"Yenteel!"

She knew she was panicking but her lungs weren't taking in air. Daybian was still lying on the ground, not having stirred despite all the activity.

"It should stop," panted Yenteel. "I put my sigil into the pattern."

"What are you saying?" said Kantees and realised she was clenching and relaxing her hands over and over. The panic made her icy inside even though she was sweating.

"I can't stop it."

Kantees looked over at Daybian's body. He must have succumbed already. Gally was sitting up but looked confused. Sheesha was stretching up and breathing deeply. Whatever was in the air must be down here and not up there. If they had something to make the air move, it might help.

"Sheesha!" she called and when he looked at her, she flapped her arms. It must have looked ridiculous. Yenteel probably thought she had lost her mind.

"Sheesha!" she called again, more insistently. And beat her arms. He looked at her with an infuriating lack of understanding. The other *ziri* looked too. It was Shingul who stood up on her back legs and, despite the lack of space beat her wings. A breeze of fresher air wafted down to Kantees and with it her panic faded.

"Yes! Shingul, that's right!" Like a maniac Kantees flapped her arms harder and faster. Shingul copied her and air began to circulate.

As if he was not to be outdone by some female, Sheesha did the same. Soon the space inside the walls was filled with beating wings and the air freshened noticeably. Kantees' tiredness left her and Gally started to laugh. Yenteel seemed to pull himself together and tried the wall again.

This time it flickered but still did not fall.

He shook his head. "I don't have the strength to reach the pattern."

On the floor, Daybian coughed and breathed deeply. Kantees knew this was temporary; eventually even this new air would be used up.

"Have you ever heard of something like this before?" she said.

"Never but I did not study in the halls of the patterners."

Of course not, he was Kadralin. If only she had been willing to stretch Sheesha instead of waiting. If only she had not been persuaded by the assurances of a man who knew nothing of the place they were in. If only she had trusted her own judgement. And now they would be killed by their own protection.

It was the milk of the Mother itself. It was not evil but so powerful it could destroy without intention.

Daybian was standing now and seemed to have understood their predicament. He pulled out his sword and struck the wall. It did nothing except hurt his hand, but he did it again anyway. And again. Kantees ducked beneath Shingul's beating wings and laid her hand on his.

"Stop."

She could see the depth of fear in his eyes. She looked at the flat blade of the sword and the end, blunted and scratched from its use yesterday as a writing tool.

She grabbed Daybian by the wrist. "Come with me."

She dragged him across the circle to Yenteel. "Can you cast the same ward on the sword?"

Yenteel frowned. "I don't …"

"This pattern." She gestured around them. "Can you put it on the sword and do whatever you do to trigger it?"

"I suppose so."

"Do it," she said. "Now."

"Charcoal will not write on steel."

"We have water."

"They won't mix."

She hesitated for only a moment and then went to Yenteel's bag and fetched his eating bowl, then took out her knife. Kneeling beside the bowl, and after only a moment's contemplation of the pain to come, she sliced the blade across her palm. Both the men made a noise of surprise, and then Daybian knelt beside her.

As her blood dripped into the bowl, he cut himself too.

Then Yenteel joined them and his blood flowed, too. After he judged they had enough, Yenteel crumbled one of his charcoal sticks into the pot and stirred it up with the knife, pummelling the lumps as he found them. The mixture thickened. Using the knife as his stylus, Yenteel inscribed the pattern around and along the sword blade.

The air was getting hotter again, and the *ziri* had given up beating their wings. They were all tired.

The process of inscription did not take very long and when Yenteel took hold of the sword hilt, Kantees put her hand on his. "Activate the ward and perhaps we can push the sword into the wall. Then you can do what you need to stop it."

Yenteel did not argue. Moments later a blue fire licked across the length of the blade. This time, it was powered by only the strength of Yenteel himself.

Together they pressed the point against the wall but still it did not want to move.

"This is my sword," said Daybian and added his hand to theirs. He pushed and the steel slid into the blue.

Moments later the wall evaporated as if it had never been, and they fell forwards across the pattern inscribed into the dusty ground.

The fresh air revived them and even though no one said anything, Kantees knew they all wanted to be away from this place. After some water and the last of the meat, having ensured the *zirichasa* were properly buckled for the journey, they took to the skies, heading west again where clouds were piling up from their grey undersides to the brilliant white tops.

Kantees was not happy. She had nearly killed them all twice over. First, with the bad decision about staying at the ley-circle, and then nearly suffocating them with the pattern she helped Yenteel create. One side of her said she could not have known that either choice was a bad one. But that was the point: She had no idea. How could she make any decisions if she did not know all the facts?

The forest streamed below them. An unending carpet of green. Then the sky filled with the clouds and a strong wind buffeted the *ziri*. They were being knocked backwards and forwards, and occasionally they would fall. As if the air was gone from under their wings.

And finally, to add insult to injury, the rain came. Not a drizzle but a downpour that soaked her through in a moment. Sheesha slowed down. Kantees knew from experience that the water just rolled off the *ziri* feathers, but it could not be easy flying through this. The air grew cold and she shivered.

The intensity of the rain increased and the world became a cocoon of grey around them. She could see neither the clouds above nor the forest below, nor anything to either side. She urged Sheesha to descend and he obeyed. A glance behind showed the others following in formation. Peering through the rain, she got the idea that Jintan was labouring. He was the oldest, after all. Would he give up or would he keep flying until his strength gave out and he simply fell from the sky?

She could not allow that to happen.

She pushed Sheesha into a sharper dive. They had been flying at the height the *zirichasa* seemed to like, which meant they were not too far from the ground—but high enough that a fall would be deadly. Still, it would not do to come down so fast that they ran into something.

She eased Sheesha back a little so the dive was less steep. The buffeting from the wind decreased as they came down.

The rain was a constant hiss in her ears but now she thought she heard something else: a rhythmic roar, not a perfect regular pattern, but one that came and went. There was a shout from Yenteel. She could not make out the words but instinctively she pulled up Sheesha's head.

The roar seemed to be behind them now.

Below them, she could see the darker grey she took for the top of the trees. And the speed with which it was moving surprised her. From the feel of the wind—and rain—on her face she had assumed they were travelling quite slowly, but the ground was rushing past.

"Too far!"

That's what Yenteel's new shout sound like. Too far? What did that mean?

She looked over her shoulder at him. He was making a big gesture with his good arm, as if he wanted her to turn round. She would have to find somewhere to land so they could talk. Had he seen such a place back there?

Pulling back on the reins again, she tried to slow Sheesha even more but he did not respond. Instead he just descended.

The tops of the trees looked wrong as they grew closer. They did not resolve into leaves and branches. The grey was a moving mass of water. The sea! And barely a *ziri*'s wingspan below them. Fear gripped her again. The Isle of Esternes bordered a sea that was so huge they might travel for days across it before encountering an island or any other land.

Yenteel had known. The sound she had heard must have been waves crashing onto the shore. The good news was that it meant they had not travelled far beyond the coastline, but she could see nothing. How could she be sure they were heading in the right direction?

The waves—more correctly, the swell—was running in towards the land. That was why she thought their speed was greater than it was. Sheesha had refused to go any slower because he would have fallen out of the sky if he had. But that meant they could follow the swell back to land. It might not be the most direct line but it should work.

She pulled Sheesha up until they were at a more comfortable height and started the turn. Not too abrupt, because the others had to follow. Yenteel had ceased to shout at her which was a relief. Once Sheesha was moving with the swell beneath, she let him have his head and he made strong strokes for the shore.

The rain continued to pour down and it was still impossible to see anything ahead. Yenteel had said the whole coastline was cliffs, which meant they would either have to climb fast or land on the beach. As long as she was prepared, that would be fine.

It wasn't long before she heard the booming of the waves. She reined Sheesha in once more. What would they land on—a sandy beach, or rocks?

A dark shape loomed out of the greyness ahead below them. She peered down, expecting to see a rock in the water but its lines were smooth curves. A sharp end curved round to the other where it was cut off. A boat!

Another, bigger, dark shape emerged.

Kantees gasped and kicked Sheesha into a climb though he was already doing it. They scraped over the top of a mast. Then boats were everywhere, there was barely an open stretch of water. They crossed a spit of land against which the sea beat its endless drum.

The rain thinned and they burst through into light under a grey sky.

Boats lined the quay, and on the stone streets people went to and fro, hundreds of them, thousands even. Houses stacked up in a great curve from left to right. Streets went up the cliffs behind in zig-zags where houses had been placed on every precarious point.

All their earlier planning of what they would do when they reached Kurvin Port evaporated like rain on a hot stone. The people of Kurvin Port turned and stared at the four massive *ziri* and their riders, who had arrived out of the sea mists.

21

They would never be able to enter the town in secret now. She turned round as far as she could so she could see Yenteel and Daybian. She was willing to take any idea now that she had messed up again. Three times in two days she could have got them killed.

Yenteel looked to be at a loss. Daybian was scanning the tops of the cliffs, and after a moment he pointed up and to the right. She looked and saw an enormous building, constructed from a reddish stone, dominating the entirety of Kurvin Port.

He could not be serious. She shook her head.

"Yes!" he shouted. "Only choice!"

She didn't want to trust him. He was one of the masters and he wanted to put them straight into the palm of the Hamalain. Without a doubt, that place was their home. The centre of their trading empire.

But he was right, they had little choice. The *ziri* were tired, and Jintan certainly could not fly much longer. If they made an attempt to go inland or along the coast, they would easily be caught. She understood what Daybian was thinking: make it look as if this was their intention, to be bold.

It was not a plan she liked, but it was the only option if they wanted a chance at finding out the truth about the raiders.

In the time it had taken her to come to this conclusion, they had passed across the coast and were climbing the steep slope. Two rivers descended from the top and bridges curved across their waters everywhere they intersected with the roadways.

It was a tremendous demonstration of engineering skill—no doubt used by the Hamalain to prove to their people they were both powerful and magnanimous. The people who lived here, perhaps even the slaves, would feel they were blessed.

She shook her head as more people came out into the thoroughfares and looked up at them as they climbed. The numbers were overwhelming. It was like a mountain of faces.

Kantees urged Sheesha to make the turn as they continued to mount the slope. Soon they reached the ridge and she could see that the town had spread into the next bay as well as extending back across lower hills with more houses of the rich.

She focused on the Hamalain house. There were gardens which they could land in but the Hamalain had a Ziri Tower, made of a different and darker stone to the rest, just like Jakalain. She could see faces looking out from the eyries. And some *ziri*. Screeches went up from the tower to be answered by those from the four they rode. She could feel Sheesha's voice through her knees. It resonated with power and she smiled at the apparent subservience of the responses from the tower.

She would have liked to land in the tower but there was no way of knowing which eyries were unoccupied. If they landed in the gardens they would have little time to get their story straight. The top of the tower at Jakalain was a landing place, so if the design here was the same as there, they could use it.

They were already over the grounds of the Hamalain estate, so she set Sheesha to climb and began a slow spiral up and around the tower.

As she had hoped, the top was flat. Gratefully, she brought the *ziri* in to land.

Daybian was unbuckled and off Jintan as fast as he could move.

"Kantees, listen, you must defer to me. If you don't, they'll have us all strung up."

"I realise that."

"Oh," he said. "You do?"

"I am not an idiot."

He frowned at her implication. "And you cannot say things like that in the presence of anyone here. Word will get back."

She nodded.

"Silence is probably the best option," he said and turned to the others. "Gally, you'll look after the *ziri* like you always do, and do what Kantees says."

"Gally always does what Kantees says."

"Yenteel, you had better be my secretary."

"And what story will explain why we are here?" said Kantees. "With almost nothing but the clothes we stand up in."

They all stood silent as the sound of shouting drifted up from below.

"Shipwreck in a storm," said Yenteel. "We escaped on the *ziri* and only just made it to land."

"I have never heard of *ziri* being taken on a boat," said Kantees. "We travel by patterners' path."

"An island without a big ley-circle," said Yenteel. "But a new source of *zirichasa*. We were coming back."

A trapdoor in the floor rattled.

"Will Gally say the wrong things?" said Daybian.

Kantees gave him a look of disgust. "He is simple-minded, *sire*, it doesn't matter what he says. We can simply deny it."

Armsmen flowed from below. Kantees gathered the reins of Sheesha and Looesa and pulled them back towards the edge. Gally had the other two.

Daybian strode forward with an air of entitlement that made the armsmen falter. Yenteel followed with a similar confidence, but a few steps behind.

"I am Lord Daybian of Jakalain. If this is the estate of the Lords Hamalain I request that I be brought into their presence so that I may apologise for taking advantage of their hospitality in this unorthodox manner."

There was only one problem with this plan, thought Kantees. One of the brothers in the house of Hamalain wanted to attack Jakalain. Daybian's announcing himself like this was a sure way to get him—and the rest of them—captured or murdered.

However, the armsmen treated him with more respect and he was allowed to descend with Yenteel, leaving Kantees and Gally on the roof with the *ziri*.

And then it started raining again. She was not entirely sure the day could get much worse.

Kantees was quietly pleased when the day improved. Having established that neither she nor Gally was armed, nor did either of them carry any weapons among their meagre supplies, the guards allowed her to talk to a Kadralin man called Ferel. He was officious and clearly unwilling to consider even the slightest possibility that her charges were of any quality—although she saw the way his eyes lingered on Sheesha.

However, they did have two empty eyries so she was able to bring Sheesha into one and the other three into the other. This arrangement was apparently the way things were done here.

"The dominant male always has his own eyrie," Ferel said. Kantees absorbed that information. Romain had never mentioned anything about dominant males. Perhaps she could learn things here. Did the people here know the *zirichasa* possessed the power of the ley-circles in abundance?

Somehow she doubted it since she herself had only discovered it by accident.

She had met slaves like Ferel before. He was the kind that liked to think they were special in some way and therefore above the others. Romain, for all his many faults, knew where he stood in the relationship between the masters and the slaves. On the inside, Ferel thought he was a master, but that was an attitude that could easily get one killed.

Kantees said nothing. She listened, agreed, and learnt, just as she had always done with Romain.

Getting the *ziri* into the eyries was a little tricky since she and

Gally were no longer able to ride. No one mentioned the fact they had arrived on *zirichak*-back. Perhaps it would be ignored. She wasn't sure.

In this instance, however, they stripped off the tack and Kantees went down through the tower to Sheesha's allocated eyrie. Then called to him. After examining the eyrie thoroughly, he settled down to sleep. She stood at the exit for a moment looking out. This side of the tower stood on the edge of the cliff and below her was not only the height of the tower but the drop-off from the clifftop past the houses to the very distant ground below. She shivered and went back inside.

She went through the same process with the other three. Looesa first to get him settled and then the other two to join him. Gally came down and for the first time in a ten-day, he seemed happy. The life of adventure was not something he tolerated easily. He preferred things to be steady and predictable. This might not have been their original eyrie but it was close enough for Gally. Romain might not be here, but Ferel could tell him what to do.

If she could have left him here with the Hamalain she would have done. If it had been her alone she would have mounted Sheesha and flown away. Avoiding masters, ley-circles, and shadowy creatures, she would have gone up into the mountains to find her people.

But it was not just her. She might not like Daybian but somehow he had become her responsibility, even if she had managed to nearly kill all of them so many times. She was the one who had got them all into the protection of Yenteel's ward. She was the one who had given them the way to escape from it. She might have got them out over the sea, but she had given them the right direction to come back.

She leaned against Sheesha. They were safe for the moment at least. And she fell asleep.

22

It was still raining outside when she woke up but it was not dark. She realised she was very hungry and imagined Sheesha probably was as well.

She went through into the back and looked at the trapdoor and ladder. She was going to have to go down at some point in order to eat and arrange for food so it might as well be now. But perhaps she could take Gally for support. He might not be useful, but he would be on her side—and that meant a lot.

The eyrie for Looesa, Shingul, and Jintan was two levels down. She found him shovelling *ziri* dung.

"Already?" she said with a smile.

He frowned. "Gally thinks Shingul has an upset tummy. The poop is very horrible."

Hardly surprising, she thought; Shingul had been eating wild food and who knew what was in it that might be bad for *ziri*. Still, she had not noticed any problem in Sheesha.

"Are the others ill?" she said.

"No, Kantees, but they have not pooped."

"We shall ask Ferel," she said. "Leave the pile somewhere off to the side. He can take a look at it." He certainly seemed better informed than Romain.

Gally had finished shovelling.

"Come on, let's find Ferel and see about some food for ourselves and the *ziri*."

"Gally is hungry, Kantees."

"Me too."

The construction of the tower seemed to be identical to the one at Jakalain, which she found odd. It wasn't just that it was a tower with eyries, but the placement of all the trapdoors, ladders, even the design of individual eyries seemed to be the same.

Just as she had seen when they arrived, the stone of the Ziri Tower was different to the rest of the Hamalain palace. It was not the red-pink stone but something darker and greyer. And older. A rebellious thought crossed her mind: What if the towers had been built by the Kadralin before the Taymalin invaded? What if this was the work of her people?

Such thought was sacrilege, of course. The Taymalin insisted the original people had been nothing more than warring tribes roaming the island. They claimed to have brought peace.

She sighed. That had been hundreds of years ago. Even if the stories they told were lies, it was really too long ago to do anything about it.

What it meant was that finding the kitchen and dining area was easy. Though her confidence at being able to find her away around was crushed when the eyes of a dozen strangers were directed in her direction. And Gally's. She searched for Ferel's face but she didn't see him; there was an older man who looked as if he might have some authority.

"Excuse me," she said.

The man looked up from the plate of tiny fish with some sort of root vegetable.

"You the ones from Jakalain."

It sounded more a statement than a question.

"Yes, I am Kantees, this is Gally."

"What do you want?"

"We hoped we would be able to feed our *ziri*," she said. "We flew far and they have not been able to eat properly in a while."

"On a ship, were you?"

"Yes, there was a storm, I think it sank."

The man eyed Gally. "Your boy doesn't say much."

"He is simple-minded but a good worker and the *ziri* like him."

"Gally looks after Looesa and Shingul and Jintan," said Gally.

The man's eyebrows rose ever so slightly, then came back down. "And you get the dominant male?"

"For seven years."

"Surprised he didn't eat you." He grinned at her, although Kantees wasn't sure if he was smiling at his joke or the thought of her being eaten.

"Sheesha is kind enough to put up with me," she said carefully. Being a keeper of the *ziri* was a job where it did not matter if one was man or woman.

"Race, does he?"

Trick question. They were only supposed to have picked him up from the island but she said she had been with him for seven years. She had already endangered them all, but perhaps she could rescue it.

"Only mock races, he has been training."

The man grunted.

"Do you think it will be possible to spare food for them?" she said again, trying to get back on track.

"And Kantees and Gally," said Gally. "Gally is very hungry."

"Hope you like fish," he said. "Just about all we get."

"Who should I speak to about the food?" said Kantees.

"Payla, over there, about your own," he said. "And me about your *ziri*. Wouldn't let one of them starve. Temekin's the name. I'm in charge of stores."

"Thank you," she said and pushed Gally in the direction of the food.

Temekin stood up and leaned in to her. "You and the others were riding."

She nodded as she looked into his face to see whether he approved or not.

"That's a death sentence."

She still could not tell if he was happy with the idea.

"Better dead later than dead soon," she said.

He nodded and then spoke even quieter. "Is it good?"

"It is the most wonderful thing I have ever experienced," she said.

His face took on a forlorn look which he replaced almost immediately. "Ever? You must still be a virgin then."

"And planning to stay that way, Temekin," she said. "Until I meet someone who's a better ride than a *ziri*, even an old one like our Jintan."

"I'd be willing to take that test."

"No offence, but I won't be looking for someone retired to the eyrie."

Then he laughed out loud and clapped her on the shoulder. "I like you, Kantees of Jakalain. I'll make sure your *ziri* get a good feed."

She thanked him, then chased after Gally who was staring at the containers, under the eye of an annoyed woman.

"Gally doesn't know this food," he said. "What will Gally like?"

"I'm sorry—Payla?"

"What's wrong with him? I tell him what will be good but he doesn't listen."

"He has the mind of a child, but he's good with *ziri*," said Kantees wondering why she had to keep excusing Galiko's behaviour. Why couldn't people just accept him for what he was? "Is there anything that's particularly sweet?"

She pointed at a plate with a white meat mixed in with a vegetable she didn't recognise.

"I'm sorry, Payla, we come from Jakalain, it's inland so we don't have a lot of fish or…" she trailed off not knowing how to describe the vegetable without insulting their host.

"Seaweed."

"Seaweed?"

"It's a plant that grows in the sea. After it's harvested, we dry it, soak it in honey, and eat it."

Kantees glanced at Gally. He hadn't reacted to the description. So she took a small amount of it and tested it. It was crunchy and very sweet. Delicious.

She offered a little to Gally. He opened his mouth warily and tasted. His face lit up in a grin.

"We'll take two of these," she said.

"Good choice," said Payla. "You wouldn't like the other one. Octopus."

Kantees had no idea what an octopus was but she was sure Payla was right. It didn't even sound nice.

The building might be the same, but the furnishings and customs were different. She did not want to make any mistakes so she found them a table off to the side that was otherwise unoccupied.

The food was strange but not unpleasant. Gally watched her before he dug into his own.

After they had eaten they climbed the tower and found the four *zirichasa* had been fed. Kantees could not tell what the food was, though it seemed to be some sort of large fish. She had no appreciation of the different types and assumed that Temekin knew his business. The *ziri* had no problem wolfing it down, except Shingul.

Ferel had declared she should be kept restrained so that she could not give whatever malady she had to the others, and that she only be fed small amounts of fish.

And at that point Kantees had nothing left to do. Back at Jakalain there were always tasks needing attention but not here, since there were others to do it. Being at a loose end made her uncomfortable.

She went to the exit from the eyrie and looked out. The rain had started up again, making it hard for her to see the town below. All she could make out were grey rooftops. Having nothing to do gave her the opportunity to worry about Yenteel and Daybian. Their story was like a house built of straw; to be honest, the only thing that gave it any validity was the fact that everyone in the town had seen them arrive from the sea.

"Kantees."

She recognised Yenteel's voice. He was panting as he awkwardly climbed up through the trapdoor, his arm not yet healed. He had been using it to help climb but slipped it back into the sling as soon as he could.

"How goes the plan?"

"Things are moving too swiftly," he said and did not sound very happy about it.

"Do they believe the story?"

"I don't know, but they are offering to send Daybian back to Jakalain using the patterner's path."

"But we can't trust them," she said.

He shook his head. Sheesha's stomach grumbled as he digested the fish.

"What if they were after Daybian all the time and I interrupted their attack?"

"They weren't after Daybian or Jelamie," said Yenteel.

"You are not going to say they wanted me." She felt the anger rising in her. She was nothing, just a slave who was good with the *ziri*. There was nothing about her that any family of the Taymalin could want.

"Not saying it does not make it any the less true."

Kantees turned away and went to stand with Sheesha. He was half asleep and did not mind when she checked the gouge in his side left by the fight. It was healing normally.

"If they had wanted me they would have attacked the tower," she said. "Or just offered to buy me. They wouldn't have been the first."

"It's possible they did not know exactly who they wanted, perhaps they just assumed it was the heir because he was Taymalin."

"I don't see how anybody could mix up a Kadralin slave with a Taymalin lord. And, in case you hadn't noticed, we're not even the same sex."

"But he is good with the *ziri*, is he not?"

For all his faults. She nodded.

"As you are."

"What have the *zirichasa* got to do with it?"

"That's something else you don't like to discuss."

"Reading the World's Pattern? Prophecies?" She almost spat the word. "We're slaves, Yenteel."

"It doesn't matter how it happened," he said. "The Hamalain and I turned up at the same time looking for someone who was good with *ziri*. I, however, had the advantage of not being blinded by preconceptions of who might be the right one."

She had no answer. She could not argue that the raid and the arrival of Yenteel had coincided.

"So why did they take Jelamie?"

Yenteel shook his head. "Because he was available?"

"But there was no ransom, they could have traded him for Daybian."

Even as she said it she knew it wasn't true. Daybian was far more important to the family than his younger brother. The lord and lady would have made the decision to lose the spare rather than put the heir at risk. So why take him at all?

She had a feeling that Daybian would not approve of that—he was here looking for his brother. *Oh, wait.*

"Daybian did not get his family's approval to come after Jelamie and us."

"He hasn't said that but no, I do not think they would have allowed it. Certainly not on his own, on the back of a *zirichak*, and an old one."

"There's nothing wrong with Jintan," she said almost absently, as if defending the *ziri* was an automatic reaction. She shook her head. Yenteel was making sense and she hated him for it. What he didn't know—and she was not about to tell him about the magic—was even more convincing.

"I don't believe it. It's just a coincidence," she said finally, hoping she might convince herself as well as Yenteel. She took a deep breath and tried to put it from her mind, there were more important matters to deal with. "How soon do they want to send him back to Jakalain?"

"They had offered to do it today."

"That's quite a rush," she said.

"Daybian demurred. And has bought us another night."

"But you think they were after Daybian?"

"Yes."

"They wouldn't let him go back to Jakalain then."

"No."

"If he was on the patterner's path, they would be able to take him anywhere they pleased."

"Quite so."

"And they think he barely escaped a shipwreck."

Yenteel pulled a face. "Perhaps. Either way they can be reasonably sure no one at Jakalain knows where he is."

"We do."

"Yes. If they remove Daybian, they will dispose of us as well."

Kantees dug her hands into Sheesha's feathers as if she was trying to draw strength from him. Where was his magic when she needed it?

"I don't know what to do," she said. "We haven't learnt anything and we're no closer to finding Jelamie."

Was there even any point in carrying on?

"Is that why we're here?" said Yenteel.

"Of course it is," she said. "Why else would I put myself at this much risk?"

"I really don't know. It seems a very strange thing to do, trying to save the life of a child you don't even like."

She turned on him. "What do you want from me, Yenteel? Do you want me to say that I am trying to make up for the wrongs I've done? Or perhaps that I was once young and in a place I did not understand where people did not treat me well, so I understand what he may be going through and want to stop it?"

"Well," he said. "Which is it?"

"Neither. Both. Honestly I do not care. I'm doing it because I'm doing it. Because if it wasn't this I would just be running with my tail between my legs. At least if I do this I can show those at Jakalain that even a slave is a human being. Someone who can choose to care for someone who might not even deserve it."

Yenteel fell silent.

It had grown dark outside. The sound of the sea carried up the cliffs and into the tower. There was a calm comfort in it. She had forgotten that sound from when she was very young. Even though she had lived so close to the water, all she really knew of it was the sound coming in through the window in the attic where she slept with the others of the household.

She supposed she had been happy then, after a fashion. The work had not been hard and she had been able to listen and learn. Though now she regretted not being able to read and write. There was so much learning in books. Perhaps, if they got out of this alive, she might persuade Yenteel to teach her.

Except he would no doubt go back to his master—she would not go with him no matter how much he pleaded. He could have Daybian instead.

"We should leave first thing in the morning," said Yenteel.

She nodded. At least this time they would not have to face the armed guards. Daybian and Yenteel could come up the tower and they could just mount the *ziri* and leave. Unfortunately they had absolutely no idea where they should be going next.

"What does it mean that we found the Hamalain dead in the pool?" she said suddenly. "The *tekrak* would have been able to cover the distance to here before we caught up with it. It could travel through the entire day without getting tired."

"I am more curious as to how it was controlled," said Yenteel.

"There was a patterner in the room beneath it," she said, surprised he didn't already know. "It was him giving the instructions to the creature."

"How do you know?"

"I saw him. They flew directly at me and then over."

"You did not mention that before."

"You did not ask."

"What else have you not told me?"

"I believe that is an impossible question to answer," she said. "The important thing is the name the raider said."

"The Dunor. Yes, well I have no idea what that is."

"We could ask the Hamalain," she said.

"I know you are not serious."

Am I not? she thought.

"The raider you spoke to," he said. "What sort of person was he?"

"None too bright and not well informed since he assumed I must be a raider as well, even though I arrived on Sheesha. Just like any of the armsmen in the castle, I suppose. Happy as long as he has something to eat, a flagon of ale, and somebody to tell him who to kill."

"Very well. Let us assume he was typical of the raiders, perhaps even one of the better ones since he had been assigned to look after the bell tower alone." Yenteel thought for a moment. "So the Hamalain who was in charge—I think it might have been the brother Lorima."

"That's what Daybian said."

Yenteel gave her a long look. "What I said about things you haven't told me."

"You were recovering from the arrow—the one I saved you from, without burning the wound."

"I believe I have thanked you for that."

"I don't think you did, perhaps it was something you haven't told me."

"Thank you for saving my life."

"What about Lorima then?"

"He's not here, away on a business trip apparently. And also overdue to return."

"So you have been making enquiries."

"Yes. The patterner would have been one of the Hamalain's own since they would not trust anyone else. No one has seen a giant *tekrak* around here so they must have acquired it, and the men, elsewhere."

"You're saying they were mercenaries," said Kantees.

"I am."

"And that they might have rebelled after the failure of the raid and decided to keep the *tekrak* and the patterner for themselves."

"It fits what we know."

Kantees considered. "Would they also keep Jelamie?"

"They might. You say he is a little wild and uncontrollable?"

"I said he's spoilt," said Kantees. "His mother had given up on having another child. There was even talk that the father might acknowledge one of his bastards just to ensure there was continuity if something happened to Daybian. So when she became pregnant again and had Jelamie …"

"She spared the rod."

"She would not gainsay him a single wish." Kantees was surprised at her own feelings over the matter. "And now he runs riot around the castle."

"So perhaps he amuses them."

"We can only hope that is the case," said Kantees. "Whatever the truth, they will not treat him as well as his mother."

She let it go at that. They could both imagine what unpleasantness could be forced on the boy.

"I must be getting back," said Yenteel. "Be ready in the morning."

"We still do not know which way to go."

"Let us think on it," he said and was gone.

Sheesha grumbled at the noise but was snoring within moments.

The dampness of the air made it cold and Kantees snuggled for warmth and comfort under Sheesha's wing.

23

"This is a completely disgusting place."

Kantees opened her eyes at the harsh voice but could see only feathers and daylight. But what she could hear were many feet on the wooden floorboards of the eyrie. Sheesha grumbled—he wasn't scared, but he was annoyed. He lifted a wing and she climbed out.

Six armsmen held crossbows pointed in her direction. Instinctively she took a few steps to the side so they were not pointing at her *ziri*.

In the middle of the men, slightly behind, was someone who could only be one of the Hamalain brothers. He even resembled the man they had found, at least in the nose. However this one was much larger—fatter. Though clearly not so fat that he could not climb the tower, but if he expanded much more that option would not be available. His clothing was of the finest quality, of course, but still practical in the form of trousers, sturdy shoes, and coat, fastened up.

She realised she had forgotten herself and immediately knelt with her head bowed. Since she had no job to be about, and the lord was here in Sheesha's eyrie, she had to pay deference to him and follow his orders.

"Seneschal."

She heard the sounds of another man moving forward, and by

lifting her head slightly she could see another pair of shoes. Also of high quality.

"Ask it where my brother is."

"Lord Trimiente wants to know what's happened to his brother."

Inside Kantees laughed. Clearly Trimiente was one of those who would not speak to a slave directly because to do so would taint him. She had had conversations like this before at the races. It was completely ridiculous.

"I do not know anything of the lord's brother."

The blow knocked her to the floor and left the side of her head aching. It was not that she had not expected it but usually it came after a repeat of the question. It would seem Lord Trimiente's patience was limited.

Kantees lifted her head to look at Sheesha who was very still. His eyes were on her. She willed him to do nothing.

The next blow slammed her head into the floorboards.

"No one told you you could get up. What do you know of Lord Lorima?"

"I do not know who that is."

The next blow landed in her side. He must have kicked her. It hurt but she had borne worse. It was just bruises, they would heal soon enough.

The seneschal's voice was in her ear. "You're thinking you can take a beating. I know. And it is true this is for show. So the lord can see you being beaten, but when we start the torture you will suffer terribly before you die. Tell us what we want to know."

"Since I am to die whether I tell you or not—even if there were something—it makes no difference if I speak or stay silent."

She felt him move away and his heel came down on her spine, knocking the wind from her, and it felt as if something broke. Through the pain there was a low growl so deep it was felt rather than heard.

"Shoot the beast," said Lord Trimiente.

"No!" The word caught in Kantees' throat and she coughed. "No."

The seneschal was back at her ear. "You care so much about the beast? Then if you do not tell his lordship what he wants to know I will have the animal strung up. Its feathers pulled out one by one. It will be flayed alive and you will be forced to watch."

The image of Sheesha being tortured formed in her mind and Kantees sobbed.

"I will tell you."

She was yanked into a sitting position and the ache in her back flared into incandescent pain. She felt the blood drain from her face and hands. The armsmen still had their crossbows aimed at Sheesha, and the seneschal was looking at her with an intensity she had never experienced. She could barely think.

"Well?"

"I will tell him."

The seneschal slapped her across the face.

"Isn't it right he should hear the words from the person who found his brother's body?"

Lord Trimiente must have been listening. "Bring it here."

Kantees could barely walk so the seneschal had to support her for the ten paces it took to approach the lord and collapse at his feet.

"Tell him."

"Let him ask me," she said. "I will be dead before the day is out. What harm is there?"

She could not see the exchange of looks between the seneschal and his lord but whatever there had been was sufficient. It was Lord Trimiente's voice she heard next.

"Where is my brother?"

"He is dead perhaps ten leagues from Jakalain."

"You're lying," said the lord but she knew from his voice he believed her.

"I found him myself face down in a pool where he had been drowned. My lord Daybian recognised him."

"So you came to seek your revenge."

"Revenge for what, lord? Your brother with his mercenaries raided our castle and though they were routed still he took something precious to Lady Jakalain, her second son Jelamie."

"Nonsense, he did not want the child."

"Nevertheless that is what happened and Daybian set off in

pursuit, but we were days behind. We came to a place where the raiders had camped and there I found the body of your brother.”

“I believe you, slave.”

A strange certainty came over Kantees. The certainty that she would die. It seemed to drive the pain from her and she breathed slower, more deeply. Then she whispered in a voice so low, no one could hear the words. “I don’t care if you believe me.”

“What?” said Lord Trimiente.

Again almost a whisper. “I don’t care if you believe me.”

She heard Sheesha move, a shuffling of his feet and wings.

“What did you say, slave?”

“I said I don’t care if you believe me.”

She pushed herself to her feet even though pain tore at her muscles.

“How dare you!”

“I dare because I am already dead and I hadn’t even realised it. You can’t do anything to me!”

With that she turned and, fighting her protesting body, she pounded towards the open exit of the eyrie.

And flung herself into the emptiness.

24

She wondered how long it would take for her to hit the ground. Since the tower stood at the edge of the precipice overlooking the town, she had further to fall than simply the height of the tower. Perhaps it would take forever, because now that she was falling she felt as if she weighed nothing, like the feathers of the *zirichasa*. It was as if she was flying. She stretched out her arms and the air streamed across her skin.

She felt guilty. She had done precisely what she said she would not do, and abandoned everyone she knew; everything she believed in. But even the guilt was blasted away by the wind of her fall.

A seabird shrieked.

Then there was a touch. And she was sucked to the side and pressed into feathers. She opened the eyes she had closed against inevitable death. *Zirichak* feathers, familiar ones. She felt his muscles move as he spread his wings and she was pressed harder into his body. He would not let her die.

Now that she could see, the houses below seemed very close and growing fast. But Sheesha bent his wings against the air and, though they still fell together at a speed that took her breath, their course bent away from the closest structures and they fell fast towards those at the base of the cliff.

But Sheesha held his wings firm and slowly their fall transformed into level flight at a speed she barely comprehended. They shot out across the sea, clearing the tops of the masts so fast she had but a moment to contemplate them before they were gone.

Then she felt Sheesha's magic: the golden glow within. It poured out and enfolded her. They were not slowing down. The sea below flashed past. The brighter crests of the swell became a blur. Sheesha was not beating his wings; instead they moved backwards until he was like an arrow piercing the world. Yet she could not feel it, cocooned within the magic.

This was it. This was their magic. This was what they did. No wonder they wanted to fly fast. It they could travel fast enough, they became arrows of the sky.

And she was the one who had brought it forth in Sheesha. If she had not thrown herself out, he would not have chased and caught her.

So she clung with her arms hooked over the front of his wings next to his body.

Then she thought of Gally, Yenteel, and—may the *Kisharuk* curse him—Daybian. He would be so jealous. If he survived the day.

"We must go back, Sheesha," she said quietly and she knew he could hear her. Perhaps not hear, but he knew what she wanted.

And suddenly Kantees found herself tumbling through the air again. And falling. She caught a glimpse of Sheesha like a ball of feathers. The magic had gone, vanished like a candle being snuffed out. The air had struck her like a solid wall ripping her from Sheesha's back.

She hit cold salty water and went under. She kept her eyes open though it stung, and clawed her way back to the surface in a panic. She did not know how to swim.

From the air the swell in the ocean had not looked very big, but now water towered over her and brought her up to its crest and then down into the trough again. She tried to shove away the panic that gripped her. People swam all the time. She knew they could do it. Anybody could do it. She desperately tried to convince herself as her head went under and she got another mouthful of water.

Where was Sheesha? Was he all right?

A shadow went over her. A giant pair of wings. He must not get soaked. He could tolerate some rain but if he was thoroughly wetted he would not be able to fly and they would both drown. Better he flew back to shore than try to rescue her.

She rose to the top of the next swell and Sheesha flew over the top of her with his legs down as if he was going to land. She knew he was not that foolish but what did it mean? She dropped down into the next trough.

In his next pass over he timed it wrong and she was at the low point. His talons splashed into the wave. She tried to shout at him to go but her mouth filled again and she just coughed. She was getting tired as she fought with the sea, and the panic was rising again. Yes it was true that she had tried to kill herself only a short time before. But she had survived and learnt so much.

She did not want to die now.

As she rose on the leading edge of the next swell she saw him coming in again, this time he glided in along the ridge of the wave itself. With perfect timing he intercepted her just as she reached the crest. His talons were again dragging through the surface and one went each side of her.

With a last effort she pushed herself upwards and hooked each arm around one leg above the claw. His wings beat and she lifted with him. They beat once more and she left the water. Again, and she was her own height above it, but looking backwards all she could see was Sheesha's sinuous feathered tail with the broad fan at its end.

He did not seem to be trying to gain much height but went round in a circle. She could see nothing but the ocean to the horizon in all directions. She did not know how long he could fly in such an unbalanced way—or how long she could hold on. There was no knowing how far they had come from the coast at the speed he had been flying.

Perhaps it was hopeless and they were both going to die anyway.

But Sheesha, after making his complete circle, set off, gaining a little height. She knew the *ziri* had excellent eyesight, far better than any human. Perhaps he had seen something she could not.

Wherever he was going, it did not take long, though she could not see where he was heading. He turned in the air again and spiralled down. The turns he made did not reveal anywhere to land—it was still water everywhere around.

She looked straight down. There was something poking up from the surface of the water. It wasn't very large and appeared perfectly round although the waves went all the way across the top of it from time to time. It did not look like rock and she did not think this was a good idea.

But she had no choice in the matter as Sheesha spiralled in for a landing. When she was a short distance above it she let go and fell. Her feet slipped on the smooth wet surface and she landed heavily. Sheesha made one more turn to make sure he knew where she was and with a flurry of beating wings landed gently.

The first thing Kantees realised was that their refuge was not fixed. It was floating and rose and fell with the water, but more sluggishly as if it was very big. This meant that every now and then its dipping down coincided with a wave, and that was when the surface became completely covered.

On the first occasion Kantees' feet were dragged from under her and she was almost swept away. However that showed her that this object floating in the ocean seemed to be a ball shape and the surface curved slowly beneath the waves.

Nor was it stone. What the outside reminded her of, most of all, was the shells she had cleaned in her first master's study. This was rougher and there were other shells clinging to it. She walked unsteadily to Sheesha who would flap into the air a little every time a big wave came over.

In a moment of stability she put her arms around his neck. "Thank you."

He brought his head round and nudged her with his snout. She took it for an acknowledgement.

"We have to get back as quick as we can," she said.

She looked at the sun. It seemed that very little time had passed since they had left Kurvin Port. She shook her head. It was confusing. So much could happen in such a short time and it seemed like forever. Yet it was nothing.

They were no safer here than they had ever been. There were plenty of things in the sea that could eat you. Her old master had smaller samples of monstrous creatures pulled from the sea by fishermen in their nets.

She had no desire to meet their larger brothers.

Kantees waited until one of the big waves had gone over the top and then climbed on Sheesha's back. This time she sat between his wing pinions with her legs down. She could grip him that way and could see. If necessary she could lean forward onto his neck.

With no further prompting from her, as their temporary refuge hit the top of a swell, Sheesha leapt into the sky beating his wings hard to quickly gain altitude. Kantees looked down. A short distance from the huge ball were five creatures floating on their backs. The scale was difficult to judge but she thought they might be about half her height. They had four legs, although their front pairs were folded like arms as they lay there watching Sheesha and Kantees climb into the sky. Their bodies were covered in fur and they had tails, big powerful ones. As the *ziri* climbed upwards they turned together and dived, heading towards the ball.

Shocalin, she thought. Legends. Yet it seemed they too were real. Intelligent as any man and renowned for their wisdom. Though, since they were only a legend how would anyone truly know how wise they were? People had thought her old master, Kevrey of Tander, was wise but she knew that trick: he said things that meant nothing—or every-thing—and let people draw their own conclusions. He might have been more knowledgeable than most but it did not make him wise. Perhaps the *Shocalin* were assumed to be wise because they said nothing.

It did not matter. It had nothing to do with her. She should simply concentrate on what was coming, and what she needed to do next. Rescue her friends and find that stupid boy, always sticking his nose into places where it did not belong.

They had to return to shore. She had no idea how far they had come so it might take all day or longer for them to return at normal flying pace. Neither did she know if it was possible to repeat what they had done before—perhaps avoiding the mess at the end. Partic-ularly if the end happened over land instead of more forgiving water.

Sheesha did not object to being sent higher. So she had him climb while heading in what she believed to be the right direction. The sea spread out beneath them, getting wider and wider. She saw a large fishing boat off to what she thought was the south but there was no sign of any land.

For one short moment she considered going to the boat and asking for directions. The thought of it made her laugh but it was not a serious idea. She knew that sailors were superstitious and there was always the risk they might try to shoot at her before she got to them.

She did not know how high she needed to go but the air was growing cold so she thought it was probably enough. The prospect of sending Sheesha into a dive back towards the water scared her, but she did not think it needed to be as precipitous a dive as when she had been falling.

He did not need to catch her this time; she just needed to be able to hang on.

"This is it, Sheesha, you're going to fly fast again."

She leaned forward. He spread his wings and went nose down into the dive. Their speed increased quickly. Soon the blast of the wind was threatening to knock her off so she leaned forward and put her arms around Sheesha's neck.

Faster and faster.

Without being told, Sheesha increased the dive angle and pulled his wings in. They were dropping like a stone. Kantees had her eyes shut against the blast. She just had to trust he would not let them crash into the sea.

Then it started. She felt the warmth boiling from him, the power, and the golden light behind her eyelids. The wind stopped and she opened her eyes. Once more they were flashing across the surface of the sea. She leaned back and Sheesha climbed. In moments they were as high as they had been before, and ahead, on the horizon, there was a dark mass.

Land, she thought and then said out loud, "Slow down."

She half expected her words to be ripped from her lips but she and Sheesha were indeed surrounded by a shell of magic that protected everything within.

This time, she got the feeling Sheesha was being more careful. Since they were enclosed, and quite high, it was difficult to tell if they were slowing down but suddenly the air ripped through. Kantees was knocked back but her legs, hooked over Sheesha's wings, saved her.

And Sheesha himself did not lose control. Instead he snapped out his wings and glided, as their speed reduced.

The mass of darker ground ahead resolved into cliffs with the mountains of Esternes in the distance. It was late afternoon when they crossed the shoreline. The only problem now, since she could not see Kurvin Port, was which direction she should head along the coast.

Unfortunately she really was going to have to ask for directions.

There was smoke rising from a bay and she decided that would be as good as any place. Once more she hoped she was not too late for the rescue. Last time she was too late to stop Jelamie from being taken. This time her companions might be dead. It depended on how the remaining Hamalain had taken her sudden escape. They might simply have killed them all in a fit of pique. Or set about torturing them. She did not know whether Sheesha's golden magic was visible —and, if it was, whether it had been observed.

One thing at a time. She could not help them—or avenge them— if she did not know which way to go.

Sheesha glided along the coast. The tide was in and waves thundered against the rocks as they went from bay to bay. It must be quite a large fishing village, she thought, because there was a considerable amount of smoke rising.

They rounded the final headland. There were boats bobbing in the bay. A pier stretched out into the water, and there were about a dozen houses. Of which all but one were smouldering ruins.

25

She circled the village once. The cliff behind was not as high as in Kurvin Port, nor were buildings built up the hill. A path led from the village up to some fields at the top of the cliffs.

She had Sheesha land at the top of cliff, and dismounted. She wanted him to stay there but she had no way of enforcing it. So she just said, "Stay here, I'll be back," and headed down the steep and rough path.

Looking up she saw Sheesha had poked his head over the edge to watch her. She stumbled on the trail and grabbed at the cliff while her stomach turned somersaults.

How can I be afraid of heights? she thought as she steadied herself by holding on to a clump of coarse grass growing out of a crack in the rock. *Maybe I'm just afraid of falling.*

She went on, this time not taking her eyes off the path. Although it was uneven, in particularly steep sections rocks had been placed to make steps. They were rounded stones, however, and were not a great help. Even so it did not take long for her to reach the flat area of the bay.

As she had been focusing on the path she looked up with surprise to see a group of men and women. Most had the pale skin of the Taymalin, though wrinkled and weathered by exposure to the sky and the sea. There was one with darker skin, though still not the shade of a true Kadralin. A by-blow of some mating between the two: a half-breed that some called Jutolin. There were plenty of them in the world, and both Kadralin and Taymalin treated them badly.

This man wore clothes similar to the rest. None of them were rich, of course.

"Who art?"

"I am of Corlain—" She had heard the family name years ago, a family not on Esternes but far to the south. "—travelling to Hamalain. What happened here?"

The man looked terrified and glanced at the others around him. If he was looking for some sort of sign, she didn't think he got one. "*Tekrak.*"

She decided to play innocent. "It's the wrong season for *tekrasa.*"

He shook his head and the other people shuffled their feet. "One *tekrak.*"

She looked at the burning buildings. "One *tekrak*? Why did you not chop off its fire-tube and pierce it through?"

He hesitated, perhaps thinking she would not believe him. "One *tekrak* bigger than a house with men riding inside."

"Men inside a *tekrak*? You have been drinking."

All the people shook their heads now. They were on his side and he gained courage. "No, one *tekrak* bigger than a house and with men in a house it was carrying."

The trouble with playing dumb was that she could not ask whether there had been a child with them without giving away the fact that she knew about it.

"There has never been a *tekrak* so big."

"So it was we thought. But the Old Mother says different. She says it is the *Slissac* returned."

Kantees wondered who the Old Mother might be. It didn't matter. What mattered was the quandary she was now in. The state of the buildings meant that this had happened recently. So the raiders could not be far away, but the longer she delayed in getting back to Hamalain the more likely she would find Yenteel, Gally, and Daybian dead.

She shook her head. This was not a quandary at all. She must rescue her friends first and with the four of them they had a better chance of rescuing Jelamie than she did alone. The speed of the *tekrak* was no match for a *ziri*, even one without magic, even if the *tekrak* didn't have to rest. And she was still unsure whether she wanted to reveal the truth to the others. Or to anyone—unless they had seen something when she escaped.

She hesitated. She needed to get back but what other secrets might the Hamalain have? Where had they found such a monstrous *tekrak*? How had a Taymalin patterner learnt to control it? How had it even occurred to him that it could be controlled? Perhaps these were important questions to be answered after all. The scholar she had served would have wanted to know. He did not like mysteries. "Knowledge is the beginning of wisdom" was one of his favourite sayings.

"Where is the Old Mother? I would like to talk to her."

The small crowd parted and the half-breed beckoned for her to follow.

He led the way between the smoking buildings. If any effort had been used to put the fire out, nothing was happening now. Most of the fishing boats were out on the water and she could see their dark shapes as the villagers fished.

"What did they want?" she said. "The men who came?"

"They took our food," he said and then choked. "And they took our daughters."

Kantees sighed. "I'm sorry."

"Will you take word of our loss to Hamalain?" he said.

"I will tell them what happened. They will take revenge on these people."

He stopped and turned. "We do not want revenge, mistress of the *zirichak*, just our daughters back."

If they have not been murdered after being raped, she thought, but did not say. There was no need, the people in the village knew why the girls had been taken. Kantees found her palms were itching. She wanted to be away, and she desperately wanted to find these raiders and let Sheesha tear out their throats one by one. There was nothing in them that was redeemable.

She knew she could not take on every woe of the world and put it right, but here the needs of these poor people coincided with her own. She would do what she could to help them.

"How many girls?"

"Five, including my Jakanda."

She did not ask how old. She did not want to know, but that they had taken the daughters meant they wanted young ones who would be too scared and too weak to fight back. Those men were base cowards.

They had left the village now and walked along the pebbled beach close to the waterline. There was a cave mouth and carved steps leading up to it. They were ancient and worn, with dips in the centre where uncounted feet had climbed through the uncounted years.

Patterns were carved around the entrance. Kantees was not curious about them, for she did not want a patterner's skills even if they could be useful. She supposed that, given the right patterns, she could control Sheesha's magic just as the *tekrak* was controlled. But she did not want that. Sheesha's power was his own. He was free to give it or not. She had no right to force it from him.

A short tunnel, with a trickle of water running along it, led inside to a large room. It was lit by a couple of candles and as her eyes adjusted she could see there was not a single surface where a pattern had not been inscribed.

The Old Mother was not that old. Kantees guessed her to be barely into her middle age and she got up without any difficulty when Kantees entered. She was Taymalin by her look.

"What is your name, Kadralin?" barked the woman.

"I am Kantees," she responded instantly, unable to hold it in.

"And you ride the *ziri* even though it is forbidden."

Kantees was not impressed. "If you know already everything about me then tell me what I want to know and I'll be on my way."

The woman grinned and gestured to the chair. "I saw you fly over and it made me curious. What is a Kadralin girl doing riding such a fine beast that could only come from the towers of a Taymalin castle?"

"It's a long story."

"I have time."

"I do not."

The woman shrugged. "What do you want to know?"

"I was told you said the *Slissac* had returned."

She shook her head. "What I said was that the *Kisharuk* stirs and the tools of the *Slissac* are abroad."

"The *Kisharuk* is a myth told to scare the children of the Taymalin."

"You think so?"

"Even if it was real, it's got nothing to do with us."

"If it was real," said the Old Mother, "do you think it would make a distinction between Taymalin and Kadralin?"

Kantees frowned and tried something else. "What tools of the *Slissac*?"

"The giant *tekrak*."

"The *Slissac* made it?"

The woman nodded and then drank from a cup she had at her side. "We are skilled with material things. But where we make machines, the *Slissac* moulded the patterns of living creatures to do their bidding."

Kantees shook her head again. "You can't do that."

"And you are so wise in the ways of patterns you can say that?"

"When Taymar escaped from the *Slissac* with his people, they would have known how to do it. But as you say, we make things, the Taymalin don't mould patterns."

"Perhaps that was a skill they were not taught. Would you teach slaves how to defeat you?"

Kantees looked away. This woman had an answer for everything, but none of it was satisfactory; after all, she was just a woman in a cave. What could she know?

"Kantees, it does not matter whether you believe me," she said. "I have answered your questions and, as you have said, you have things to do."

Kantees stood up and felt that she had been very selfish. "Is there anything I can do to help?"

"Just do what you have to do."

"I need to get to Hamalain," she said. "Which way is it?"

The woman pointed and then dropped her arm. Kantees desperately tried to determine which way that was in respect to the coast.

She kept it in her head as she stepped back through the tunnel and into the light: to the northeast.

"Sheesha!" she called as soon as she was on the beach and could see his wings poking up over the edge of the cliff. His long neck poked up. "Come on!"

The *zirichak* launched himself over the cliff and snapped his wings out. In moments he was gliding over her head at speed. He whipped into a turn that also killed his speed and landed on the beach.

She turned to the man. "What is your name?"

"Welyn."

"I promise I will search for your daughter and try to bring her back to you."

If I don't, I'll be dead.

She climbed on to Sheesha's back and settled herself between his wings. "When the giant *tekrak* left, which direction did it go?"

The man pointed in the other direction to Hamalain, which made sense because if they knew where they were they would not want to go that way. They would probably make their way along the coast raiding as they went. Until they were stopped.

She launched Sheesha into the air and set him on the course along the coast, encouraging him to make the best speed he could—without using the magic.

Once more she seemed to be heading into trouble to perform the impossible. That appeared to be the entire story of her life, now. So perhaps she had better learn to enjoy it.

The chances of her ending up dead were increasing all the time.

26

The Ziri Tower at Hamalain came into sight like a finger pointing accusingly at the sky. And she had no plan. The sky was overcast, but the clouds were high and visibility was good, which meant she could be seen easily as she approached. It was not close to evening, so if she wanted to enter when it was dark she would have to wait. She did not think she could afford the time.

Trying desperately to think of how best to get into the castle, she put Sheesha into a climbing spiral. There was no way she could use the magical speed that he could achieve; he would simply overshoot. And besides, she did not want to reveal that—assuming the Hamalain did not know already.

Then she heard the strange, deep hoot of a *zirichak*. It came from the far distance but was unmistakable. She knew it must be Shingul or one of the others, because she had never heard a *ziri* utter that sound until this journey. Any *zirichasa* that lived in a tower did not use it.

She peered towards the tower itself but could not make out anything. Sheesha, however, was not looking that way. He had pulled out of the spiral and his neck was pointing inland at Kurvin Port. There was no dust trail but she could see three wagons on the road, carrying *ziri*—one in each. Sheesha immediately headed that way but Kantees leaned back and pulled on his neck feathers.

"No, Sheesha, wait."

She stared down and saw armsmen surrounding the carriages, and men who might be Yenteel, Gally, and Daybian. Out in front, riding horses not *kichesa*, was a group of men she did not recognise.

They must be heading for the ley-circle of Kurvin Port, intending to walk the patterner's path to somewhere—and it would not be to Jakalain, of that she was certain. Despite it being the place of her slavery, right at this moment, even Kantees would be happy to be back there. As long as they weren't planning to put her head in a noose.

She looked along the roadway they were following. It ended at a circle—except the circle was a hole in the ground. She recognised it from the few times they had raced at Hamalain. Ley-circles were often not on the surface. They might be below it, and many were underwater. The capital city of Canvor in Faerholme, far to the south on the mainland, was famous for having a powerful ley-circle that lay below the level of the lake by which it stood, which meant the city could only be approached by land and thus never be surprised.

Hamalain's was below the ground. She could see the road led to a ramp and down.

Sheesha was becoming more insistent. He wanted to go but she managed to hold him in check. The group would reach the ramp quite soon. She urged Sheesha to turn and fly around to approach the circle from the other side.

The best moment for attack would be just before the pattern for the path was woven. She had travelled enough times by the path she knew it would take a little while to complete the pattern but beyond knowing it would be "soon" she had no real idea.

The riders at the front of the group dismounted and walked down into the tunnel. The *ziri*, however, were taken down on the carriages. It was unlikely they would transport the wagons as well, so there would be a short time while the *zirichasa* were unloaded.

The *ziri* would not have their saddles or reins, so everyone would have to ride without. Daybian would be fine once he had finished complaining. Gally would not like it but would do as she said, and Yenteel—well, he would just have to put up with it.

Kantees counted to fifty, slowly, after the wagons disappeared to give them a chance to get down to the ley-circle proper. She leaned forwards and Sheesha, no longer restrained, went into a dive.

The angle was not sharp so his speed did not reach the point at which the magic became active. She did not know how deep the circle was and she wanted to arrive with as little warning as possible. The nature of the ley-circles made them indefensible close up. It was only possible to build walls at some distance out from them, and it seemed the Hamalain had not even bothered to do that.

She remembered one city they had gone to on Esternes that had created massive fortifications around their circle. The circle itself was not large but the city was the centre of mining. Metals were constantly being shipped out and luxuries brought in. The family that owned the place, the Garbalain, were richer even than Hamalain and clearly they feared attack.

Sheesha arrived over the hole, driven through the rock by the Mother's feeding. It was deep, perhaps almost half the height of the Ziri Tower. And that meant she had arrived too soon. She had forgotten how much time it took to get down to its base, via the cavern.

From off to one side, in the direction of the road, came shouting —and it was not friendly. Armsmen were already hurrying her way. She groaned. This time she really could get them all killed.

"Down, Sheesha, quick."

The *ziri* turned into one of his descending spirals. He seemed to understand the need for speed and was descending at a tight angle. One of the armsmen had a bow and he was drawing an arrow as Sheesha and Kantees went below the level of the ground.

She looked down to where dozens of candles, mounted on massive candelabra, lit the space. Three men, patterners by their robes, were talking and pointing at the ground. Discussing their patterns, no doubt.

She half expected arrows to rain down on her and Sheesha as she looked up to see the armsmen's heads silhouetted against the grey sky. But they did not shoot.

Instead she heard them calling down, warning the men below of the descending *zirichak*. The patterners looked up when she was almost halfway down. The width of the circle was barely sufficient to accommodate the breadth of Sheesha's wings.

The words "Take cover" floated past her as a warning to those below. The armsmen were holding their fire for fear they might hit the patterners. Kantees urged Sheesha to descend faster and he did something she had never seen.

He stopped circling and put out his wings, bent upwards. Together they almost fell towards the ground. Small wingbeats and adjustments to the angles kept their motion under control but they were going down vertically. Moments later they hit the bottom.

An arrow splintered on the ground next to them.

There was a single large arch which was an entrance to a tunnel. It was very rough and the edges looked melted. She leapt from Sheesha's back. "Come on!" she yelled as two more arrows barely missed them. Just one through a wing could prevent him flying.

In his ungainly way, he followed as she jumped through the opening—it was easily big enough for the *ziri* but the ground was uneven. She wondered how often they had to remake the entrance after a feeding had distorted the rock. Once inside, it was impossible for the archers above to hit them. In the tunnel she noticed an acrid and unpleasant smell that bit into her nose and throat.

The tunnel, and its rising floor level, was well lit with lanterns fixed to the walls. This far in, the magic would not touch them so permanent features could be placed safely. She knew she needed to move quickly, otherwise the patterners would give too much warning and she would be captured. Moments later there was a bend in the tunnel and beyond it she emerged into an open space. A staging area. The carts were being unloaded at the other side.

But the panting patterners were already shouting a warning, their voices echoing round the stone walls of the chamber.

"Daybian! Yenteel! Gally!" she yelled. "Shingul! Looesa! Jintan!"

And Sheesha roared deafeningly. Kantees felt as if the noise shook the very stones around her. She would not have been surprised if the daggers of rock hanging from the ceiling dislodged and fell.

Across the middle of the space, the towers of stone one expected to see had been destroyed and removed, leaving only lumps. But around the walls it was like a construction of some mad architect with multi-coloured columns—some ribbed, some smooth—reaching up from the floor to the ceiling.

Sheesha's roar did have one effect. The air was filled with the screechings of thousands upon thousands of *sikechasa*—which explained the smell—that exploded into the air like a storm, wheeling and turning, filling the whole space with their noise and fluttering. Yet not a single one of them touched her as she ran across the stone floor.

Men were shouting, some in fear, others in anger. She could hear someone trying to give orders to get things under control. There was a sharp *crack* from one of the carts: the shattering of wood. She glanced round to see Daybian smashing his forehead into the nose of a guard who seemed more fearful of the wheeling *sikechasa* than of the prince until the pain made him lose interest in everything else.

Yenteel and Gally were on the ground. Gally lay face down, whimpering in terror while Yenteel tore at the cords around his wrists with his teeth. The *sikechasa* were escaping through both tunnels and the air was clearing of them.

One of the carts collapsed as its axle snapped. Looesa stretched upwards and the binding ropes slipped from him. Behind Kantees, someone screamed and then went silent with a cracking of breaking bones. She chose not to look but focused on Daybian.

He was trying to get the knife from his prone assailant.

She pushed him out of the way. "Let me!"

Since her hands were free she was able grab the fellow's blade from his belt in a trice. She turned and grabbed one of Daybian's wrists to keep him still while she sawed through the leather thongs. One went, then another, and the cords fell away from him.

"Help Yenteel and Gally," she said into his ear. "I'll get the *ziri*."

He didn't argue. He didn't even pause but grabbed the armsman's sword and went. Looesa's jaws were clamped around the arm of one of the soldiers, who was whimpering in terror. Kantees looked away, she did not want to see.

Shingul was struggling in the cords that bound her wings to her body, the feathers protecting the flesh beneath from the coarseness of the ropes. Kantees could not imagine how much power Looesa had been able to bring to bear to snap his cart. That power now made the poor armsman scream as an accompaniment to sounds of bones crunching and flesh ripping.

"Lay still, Shingul," Kantees said quietly and the beast stopped struggling immediately. Kantees attacked the cords binding her neck. One at a time she hacked through them until they were loose enough for Shingul to raise her head.

As Kantees moved to attack the ropes on her body, Shingul's neck doubled over on itself, zipped over Kantees' shoulder, and snapped at something that screamed and then went silent. A sword clattered to the floor beside her.

Kantees concentrated on the ropes while Shingul's head hissed and weaved above her. Finally enough were gone and Shingul lifted herself up. She roared the way Sheesha had. Kantees could feel her anger like a wave of heat.

She looked up to see Yenteel and Gally working on Jintan's bonds. She could not help there. Daybian ran an armsman through with the sword and, as he turned and pulled the weapon from the man's belly, she saw the grim concentration on his face.

Then he noticed her watching him. She fully expected him to grin —but instead he lifted his sword before his face in salute. A *ziri* crunched something or, more likely, someone behind her.

And it was abruptly quiet.

27

"This respite will be momentary," said Daybian, his voice calm and low.

Kantees had never seen this side to the man before. He was deadly serious, so unlike the cocksure princeling she knew.

"We must go," he said. "They will return in greater numbers."

"Perhaps they will flee," said Yenteel. "I would, and not return."

Even Kantees knew that was wishful thinking.

"Gally does not like it here. Gally wants to fly away."

"Yes," said Kantees. "You give us wise counsel."

He grinned although she was sure he had no idea what her words meant.

At that moment Sheesha's head turned towards the main entrance and he growled. The other three followed suit. The enemy were coming.

"This way," said Kantees and headed at a jog back towards the ley-circle. "We can fly out."

From up the tunnel the sound of boots on stone grew like distant thunder. She and her companions ran faster but had barely reached the exit when the armsmen exploded from the other tunnel with a shout.

Kantees paused at the entrance to make sure Yenteel and Gally went through.

"Keep going, it only goes to the circle," she said. The armsmen were taking up position behind the shattered carts and debris. The whirring of an arrow startled her, but it was going away from them. Turning to see Daybian nocking another, she blinked. She had not even seen him pick them up.

The second arrow whistled away as Sheesha brought up the rear of the *ziri*.

"You go," said Daybian. "I can hold them off for a short time."

Kantees could see the five arrows at his feet. A very short time. An incoming arrow shattered as it hit the wall above the exit.

"They're as bad as me," said Daybian.

"Don't get yourself killed," she said.

He fired. Four arrows. "So you *do* care about me."

"As much as I care for any sad and pathetic animal. Oh!" An arrow grazed her arm, drawing blood.

"Love to chat," said Daybian. He fired. Three arrows. "But you have some other sad and pathetic animals to look after."

She turned away from him and hurried down the tunnel, feeling like she was never going to see him again. And for some reason, that made her chest hurt.

She picked up the pace. He only had a couple of arrows and while they might be cautious crossing the cave it wouldn't take them long. But all she and the others had to do was get on the *ziri* and fly out of here.

When she got to the bottom of the tunnel she had to push her way through four *ziri* and two humans crammed by the door.

"What's wrong?"

"Archers," said Yenteel and pointed up.

She cursed herself for an idiot. Of course. They weren't stupid; they would have surmised the plan and put men on guard.

"To the *Kisharuk* with them," she said and ran out into the circle.

There were three sets of candelabra. Before an arrow hit the ground she knocked the first one over, she had come out so fast and unexpectedly. She reached the second and that went over, too. Most of the candles went out as they hit the ground. The archers couldn't hit what they couldn't see. But they would have realised what she was doing and if they had any sense they would be aiming for the third one, waiting for her to appear.

She didn't stop moving but breathed a prayer to the Mother and then screamed as she ran at the third. Pain ripped through her leg as she struck its heavy metal stem and knocked it down. She fell in the other direction but kept rolling despite the pain, hoping to disappear into the shadows available.

She did not die.

Not yet.

But there was no time. Daybian would be out of arrows by now but he would stay there, pretending he was still able to shoot, to slow them down. He was an idiot too. They were well-matched in that way.

"Come out, quickly. Stay to the sides."

Yenteel and Gally emerged. Light came down from above, of course, and Kantees found it hard to believe that the people up there could not see them easily. But no arrows flew. They would be waiting for the *ziri* to come up, when they would be easy targets.

And they were right to do so; there was no way they could miss a bunch of giant flapping dragons. For a moment she contemplated returning to the cavern, but in that space the *ziri* would not be able to fly and could be picked off easily.

"Look," she said to the other two as Sheesha strode out into the circle. "We can ride without a saddle and reins." Sheesha stooped and she flung a leg over his neck. "We sit where the saddle would be and hook our legs under the wings like this."

"How can you guide them?" said Yenteel.

"You lean forwards, back, left, and right. They understand what's needed but mostly you just have to give them a direction and let them do it. You don't have to control their every movement."

She looked at Jintan. She expected he would just follow the rest, leaving Daybian behind.

"There will be archers at the top," she said. "Sheesha and I will go first and draw their fire."

"I'm sorry I have no pattern I can work to help," said Yenteel.

"Nobody has a pattern for this," she said.

But we are on a ley-circle, she thought. *It may not be the most powerful in the world but beneath us lies the power of the Mother's milk.*

She leaned forwards and put her arms around Sheesha's neck. In the distance she could hear fighting. They had reached Daybian. Very soon they would be here.

"Sheesha," she said quietly to him. "The power is here. Can we not use it, my love?"

She imagined she felt the power of the *zirichasa* and imagined the milk beneath them that did not lie quiet. It was a roiling lake, bubbling and steaming gold, desperate to be free. The raw power from which patterns were made, waiting to be shaped. Why not shaped by the *ziri*?

"Up, Sheesha!"

He burst into the air and stroked hard upwards. Faster and faster. The light grew.

And turned golden.

It was almost as if they jumped directly into the sky. She knew she should have fallen but there was no sensation. The light blinked away and for a moment they were falling. Kantees hung on as Sheesha regained control. They were above the hole, at least the height of the Ziri Tower.

Without a word from Kantees, Sheesha screamed and dived.

The well of the ley-circle was surrounded by armsmen, not a great number but plenty enough to shoot *ziri* in a barrel. But they were not peering into the well. They were staring up at Sheesha as he roared from the sky directly at them.

Kantees could barely look as the first half-dozen were knocked into the well. And, while Looesa and Shingul made their way from the depths, the archers ran from the winged monster, their weapons forgotten as this sky-demon that had shot from the well, bathed in golden light, came roaring at them.

Not a single arrow was fired.

Kantees saw Looesa and Shingul emerge into the light but Jintan was not following.

Kantees oriented herself and pointed back along the coast. "Yenteel! Follow the coast until you come to a village that is burning. Wait for us there."

He nodded and awkwardly managed to get Shingul turning.

Sheesha needed no encouragement to dive back into the hole. Kantees came down slowly, she did not want to collide with Jintan on the way up.

The words "Jintan, up!" echoed from below and Kantees grinned in relief. Daybian was too stupid to die.

Then there was a cry of pain—not human. "Jintan! Come on, you can do it."

"Daybian!" shouted Kantees.

"Come on, Jintan, old warrior!"

"Daybian!"

Kantees couldn't see anything. She urged Sheesha lower but he was reluctant. What could he see that she could not?

"Ah! Get off me, you brute." Daybian.

All she could hear was hissing and snapping which ceased abruptly. An arrow arched up and over Sheesha before falling back. She could have snatched it from the air if it had been closer.

"Daybian!"

"I'm all right, Kantees. Jintan …" His voice broke off. "Don't come down. Too many."

Then there was another thud and he said nothing more.

Kantees held in her grief.

"Sheesha, go."

Strong wingbeats carried her up and out.

2 8

She was crying for Jintan, not Daybian—she didn't even like him much. The world was a damp blur and she barely knew the right direction. But Sheesha did. Did Sheesha grieve for Jintan? She could not tell, but if she worried for someone else she could push her own sorrow away.

This time she had succeeded in getting one of them killed.

The others, especially Daybian, would say that it was not her fault. But she was in charge, although she was not entirely sure how that had happened. Perhaps if she had been willing to let Daybian lead they wouldn't have got into this situation. *Perhaps*.

And now Jintan was dead. He was old, of course, but that was not the reason his body lay at the bottom of the well getting cold. She was. If she hadn't been so foolhardy this morning—was it only this morning? If she had not tried to kill herself and leapt from the tower, then Sheesha would not have saved her and she would not have been carried away by him.

Daybian would have been taken off to wherever the Hamalain were taking him. Perhaps they would have taken her as well. She did not want to admit that Yenteel was right. If they had followed *that* course she, Gally, and he would be dead and the *ziri* would be living in the Hamalain tower.

Instead they were all alive save for one *zirichak*.

That did not make it all right. She cared more for the *ziri* than any of the people, except perhaps Gally. The loss of Jintan hurt her like a thousand torments.

But this was no time to be maudlin. She needed to focus. They may have lost Jintan and Daybian but she had a good idea of where the *tekrak* was and where it was heading. While it was clearly possible to make a *tekrak* fly at night, it was still a plant and she doubted it liked to travel in the dark. Plants wanted light, and especially sunlight. That was why they flew as high as possible when they travelled the skies in spring and autumn—to stay above the clouds—and why they landed at night. To feed and to rest.

And they were now just a day behind it and its handlers (or was it its crew?), and the *ziri* could fly faster than a *tekrak*. The only question was which direction the enemy had taken.

The wind had dried her tears. She took Sheesha up so that she could see further. Hopefully, his superior eyesight would spot the other two soon. They needed her direction.

The smoke of the burned village came into view and she set Sheesha to descend. She heard the deep, hooting calls of Looesa and Shingul as they caught sight of Sheesha. It made her smile. Below she could see them on the top of the cliff with their wings outstretched, two figures standing near to them.

And at what cost had she rescued them? The armsmen would tell their masters how the *ziri* had shot like a golden arrow from the ley-circle and at such a speed they could not possibly have fired on it. Then the Hamalain would know that their search had been successful, even though they had lost their brother. Just as Yenteel no doubt did. He could be smug in the knowledge that he had chosen the right person to attach himself to.

But, she thought, *it's not me. It's Sheesha.*

"Gally rode Looesa without a saddle, Kantees," was the first thing he said to her after she slipped from Sheesha's back to the ground. She put her arm around his shoulders and gave him a hug. "And you were like a flower!" He grinned widely.

She frowned. "A flower, Gally? I am not like a flower."

"A yellow flower growing very fast."

Then she laughed. Of course. "Yes, I suppose I was."

"I am also interested in how you became a flower," said Yenteel, and he was not smiling at all. "Very interested indeed."

"Where is Jintan?" said Gally.

Kantees froze. How could she explain to Gally? She looked at Yenteel and the look on her face must have told him everything.

"Daybian?" he said.

"I'm sorry, Gally, but Jintan was hurt by the armsmen when he tried to escape with Daybian."

"Is he killed?"

Kantees was not sure whether he meant Jintan or Daybian.

"Daybian is alive, I think." She stopped with the lump in her throat threatening to steal her words. "Jintan was killed." Her voice came out in a croak that could barely be heard.

"Poor Jintan," said Gally. "Gally thinks he would have liked to be like Sheesha's flower."

Kantees turned away to face the sea. Her throat hurt, and the grief was like heavy clouds in her eyes. She did not trust herself to speak without sobbing and she did not want to do that in front of Gally and Kantees.

As she faced away from them, trying to get control of herself, a group of the villagers appeared over the top of the cliff. She recognised Welyn, and wondered why he was chosen to speak to them. Was it because their skin colour was the same? Did people really care out here, even though Welyn lived among them and had even had a wife and child? People were strange.

She was more surprised to see the Old Mother. For some reason Kantees had it in her head the woman would stay in her cave, weaving patterns to ensure a good harvest of fish, and healing the sick.

So Kantees swallowed her grief and brushed the tears from her eyes, and when they arrived she introduced them: Welyn first, and then the Old Mother.

"She's not old," said Gally.

"My name is Lintha," she said to Gally. "I am not old, but I am older than you. So you can call me Mother."

There was something about her that made Gally stare and then realise he was staring, for which he had been punished in the past, and he looked away.

"Old Mother," said Yenteel. "I am honoured to be in the presence of one so revered and wise."

She looked slightly amused. "I suspect you are a man with a sly tongue."

Yenteel did not smile but looked her in the eye. "Everything I have is at your disposal. Even my tongue."

Kantees was shocked and outraged on the woman's behalf, but she just laughed.

"If I require your service, I will send for you. But I doubt there is anything you can do for me."

"I am well travelled and have learnt much. I am happy to be a teacher as well as a student."

At which point Kantees became confused. From what Yenteel had said back at the castle, she assumed he preferred the company of men. Yet here he was, flirting with the wise woman of the village.

She interrupted. "We have important matters to deal with."

Yenteel had the decency to look embarrassed.

"You intend to go after the raiders?" said Lintha.

Kantees nodded. "They have the son of the Jakalain, and your daughters." She glanced at Welyn's face as she said it; he mirrored her own grief, though she could not imagine what it must feel like to lose one's own flesh. She had no one but the *ziri*.

"If you are able, then we will be forever in your debt."

"You are Taymalin and we are nothing but runaway slaves. You will owe us nothing."

Lintha smiled. "You think I am Taymalin because my skin is pale? My father was as dark as Welyn, and he was the leader of the village for most of his life. Just as Welyn is now—why do you think he is the one who speaks with you? My mother was dark too, but her mother had been of the Taymalin—as much as we care about such things— and I take from her. It is only in the cities that those in power make distinctions based on skin. We cannot afford to. Our blood is the same colour and our sweat tastes the same. It is only by our blood and sweat that we live.”

Kantees was not sure what to say. She felt she owed them an apology, but to give one would reveal the depth of her own prejudice—inherited from the masters. So instead she went back to the point.

“Can you help us?”

“We can give you food and a place to sleep for the night that is out of the wind.”

“And the *ziri*?”

“There are caves large enough.”

“I would sleep with the *ziri*,” she said. “And so will Gally.”

“I’ll take a bed,” said Yenteel.

Lintha gave him a sidelong glance. “We will see what can be arranged. Our houses are barely habitable and it will take a while to put them back in order. The fishing must always take precedence.”

The wind had increased and was blowing the feathers of the *zirichasa* every which way.

And then rain hit them. Freezing cold, from off the sea.

Kantees, Gally, and the three *ziri* were housed in a cave that was used for storage and stank of fish. But it was deep and well out of the rain. Dry wood was brought for them to build a fire. The cave became smoky but not so bad that they couldn’t sleep.

Yenteel, as he had said, did not sleep in the cave. Kantees suspected he might be with the Old Mother, and shook her head. It seemed inappropriate somehow and still a little confusing. So instead she worried about Daybian. She hoped he had not been killed, but she was determined to find him anyway. Then she would avenge or rescue him, whichever it happened to be.

Then she thought of Jintan, and cried into Sheesha’s feathers.

29

Breakfast involved bread and eggs. Kantees was grateful it wasn't fish, though she suspected fish was brought out for meals most of the time. The fields at the top of the cliff did not look as if they provided more than a meagre supplement for the main product. The bread was old and hard, since the ovens had been destroyed in the fires, but the eggs flavoursome.

Yenteel joined them when she and Gally had almost finished, but he did not want any of their food. He looked tired. Kantees shook her head slightly, and went back to finishing the mess of eggs on the stone that served as a plate.

"Did you receive any divine inspiration as to where we should go?" said Kantees in a tone that was more cutting than she had intended when the words were in her head.

But Yenteel did not seem to notice. "Along the coast."

"Gally likes the eggs."

Yenteel spoke before Kantees had a chance. "That's good, Gally, make sure you eat them all up, too."

Kantees frowned at him. Did he think he was going to usurp her authority over Gally as well? She was almost tempted to tell him about the *ziri* magic. Just to show him she was still in charge.

It was almost as if he read her mind. "Are you going to explain about what you and Sheesha did yesterday?"

"I don't know what you mean."

He turned and looked at her. He might have been tired but she felt as if he was attempting to pull the very thoughts from her mind. Honestly, she didn't know why she was being so contrary. Only that she was irritated with him.

"Magic, Kantees."

"No."

"Yes, it was magic. I felt it. You said you don't know any patterns."

"I wasn't lying."

"We are all aware of how accomplished a liar you are. Please do not prolong this."

"I'm not lying," she said. "I don't know patterning. I don't want to know. You can keep your precious secrets."

"It's not my secrets I'm concerned about, it's yours. You and Sheesha shot out of that well like an arrow from a bow," he said. "We would have ended up like one of those urchins in the sea if you had not been able to get out."

She knew about urchins. She had seen them with and without their spines at the scholar's house. Then her eyes widened, as a realisation came upon her: the vast ball she and Sheesha had landed on. It had been like an urchin's shell.

It was crazy. How could an urchin have grown that big unless it was an abomination? Did that mean that a *nachak* as big as a mountain might truly stalk the heart of Esternes? Everything she had thought were legends became revealed to her as she travelled.

"What?" said Yenteel.

She realised she had become silent and withdrawn into her thoughts, even though he had been talking to her.

"I'm sorry, Yenteel. I should have told you but I barely even believed it myself even though I was there and saw it happen." Because, when you are a slave, secrets are the one thing that you can keep and no one can steal them away.

"Tell me what?"

She shook her head. "First you must explain something. When you were in the cell you said you would have spent the night with the soldier if he had wanted—rather than having him lock you up."

"I did say that."

"I believed you."

"It was not a lie."

"Then tell me you did not spend the night with Lintha last night."

He smiled. "But, Kantees, I did lie with the Old Mother last night."

"I don't understand. I know that some men prefer the company of other men. I thought you were one of them, yet"—she threw her hands up—"last night?"

"Have you never observed beauty in another woman?"

"Yes, but that's not the same. All women are more beautiful than I …" She hesitated. "Except Hogoma. And that's not her fault."

"Did I meet her?"

"You would remember. But it's not the same, Yenteel."

"Not precisely, no," he said. "But have you ever felt attraction to a man?"

She knew the answer only too well. "I don't know what you mean."

"Do lies always come so readily to your lips?"

She sighed, and lied. "Yes, I have."

"Then just imagine that you might also feel that for a woman as well as a man."

"I don't."

His smile changed to a mischievous grin. "Are you lying to me again?" She frowned and he laughed out loud. "I am only teasing you."

"So you would lie with a man or a woman?"

"I believe I have said so," replied Yenteel.

"Do you want to lie with me?"

"What a fateful question," he said. "Consider if I were to say no, then you would be affronted and upset. You would think there was some fault with you. Yet if I were to say aye, you would be threatened and disgusted. And try to push me away. There are some questions, Kantees, it is not wise to ask."

"So you don't want to?"

"And there you have it. I cannot even be equivocal because you instantly jump to the negative. This is a conversation, Kantees, that neither you nor I can win. Let us return to the real question, shall we?"

She was annoyed he had not answered her, regardless that she understood the logic of why. She took a deep breath and tried to put it aside.

"I was not lying when I said I did nothing. It was Sheesha that did it."

Yenteel glanced across at the *ziri*. Kantees followed his gaze. Sheesha was leaning over a rock pool staring into it intently, his whole body still—not relaxed, but rigid as if he was holding himself ready. His head lashed down into the water, which erupted in a great splash. He came back up with something wriggling between his razor teeth. Then he sneezed and his prey disappeared back into the pool.

Sheesha shook himself to get rid of the water, which sprayed from his head and neck feathers. He looked around for his lost meal but couldn't see it.

"Sheesha did the magic?" said Yenteel.

"People do magic, animals *are* magic," said Kantees.

"And nobody has discovered this before?"

Kantees shrugged. "I don't know. Perhaps it was forgotten."

Yenteel nodded. "Things do get forgotten."

She looked out, past Sheesha, at the sea and to the horizon. "It happened yesterday." *Was it truly only yesterday?*

"Yes, I am curious about yesterday too. How was it you escaped?"

She hesitated. She had been in such a strange place in her mind when Trimiente had questioned her. "I …" She wanted to lie, wanted to say that she had leapt onto Sheesha's back to fly to freedom. But if that had been the truth, she would never have discovered the magic.

"I tried to kill myself by throwing myself out of the tower." The words came out all in a rush and tears ran down her cheeks. "I'm so sorry. They were threatening Sheesha, they would have hurt him. It was the only thing I could do to save him."

Yenteel moved closer and put his arm around her shoulders. She tensed at his touch but then dropped her head onto his shoulders and sobbed.

"That was very brave," he said after a while.

"It was stupid," she said. "I deserted you all."

"If you did it to save Sheesha, then that is brave. It may not have been the most intelligent thing to do, but it was not cowardly."

He let her cry more and then said, "However, you are here crying on my shoulder so somehow you managed not to die. That sounds like an interesting story."

So she told him how Sheesha had come down after her, and prevented her from being dashed against the rocks and houses. And how he had sped away as his magic took hold. She told him about the giant urchin shell and the *shocalin*. Yenteel was impressed at that.

After she had described the return journey, he listened to how she had begun the rescue, at which point he knew the rest.

"But how is it Sheesha could fly fast so quickly in the rescue?"

"The circle," she said. "It was the same as when you used the one in the forest for your pattern. I thought perhaps Sheesha could use it, and he did."

"Using the power from the forest ley-circle was your idea," said Yenteel.

"But it worked."

"Yes, and you suggested it to Sheesha, didn't you? Just as you did me?"

"Don't be foolish, *ziri* don't understand language."

"So how was it you explained your idea to him?"

Kantees opened her mouth to answer and then closed it again. It had not occurred to her, everything had happened so naturally.

"Do you think the others can do it?" said Yenteel.

"The other *ziri*? I don't know but every *tekrasa* can fly and has a fire-tube, doesn't it?"

He nodded. "If it truly is part of their nature then they would all be capable." He looked at Looesa and Shingul. "But perhaps they lose the ability with age."

"Sheesha did not seem exhausted by it," said Kantees. "But it was only for a very short time, I suppose." And then she stood up as if she wanted to put an end to the conversation. "We should go. We have Jelamie and five girls to rescue."

"Have you given any thought to that?"

"I have not," she said. "But let us find them first."

30

antees sent Gally to find Welyn and inform him they were leaving. He returned with a group of villagers and the Old Mother.

Welyn gave them a couple of sacks filled with dried and smoked fish with some bread. Kantees was genuinely grateful though she was more concerned about feeding the *ziri*, or at least giving them an opportunity to feed that did not lose them too much time.

Lintha gave Yenteel several pieces of rolled-up bark and a kiss on the cheek. "They are for mist and for rain," she said, "and another for wind; you may find them useful when your other magic lets you down."

Yenteel seemed touched. Kantees assumed they must be patternings. He must have been a good lover, she thought. Or Lintha hadn't had it for a long time—it probably wasn't good to indulge with the villagers themselves. She told herself off for being so harsh. Lintha did not deserve bad thoughts.

"Come on," she said impatiently. "The sun is climbing."

The *zirichasa* lay down so the three riders could climb on easily, and then stood up on their hind legs. Kantees gave a short wave and gave Sheesha a little kick.

A flurry of wings brought them up to the level of the cliff. Kantees gave Sheesha a direction along the coast away from Hamalain. The villagers were lost to sight almost immediately. Kantees debated how they should proceed. Staying low along the coast did not seem best. They wanted to be able to approach the *tekrak* without being seen. So it was a choice between going out to sea, or going high.

She glanced up. It was fully overcast but the clouds were not low and it didn't feel as if it would rain today.

If she were a raider, she would be more concerned at being followed or attacked by land. The sea would not be considered a threat. So if their assumptions were correct and the raiders were following the coast, it would be best to be over the sea. *And* high.

Sheesha curved out over the water, gaining height, and the other two followed in their perfect formation. Kantees looked behind. She missed seeing Jintan there. She missed having Daybian to complain about.

One thing at a time, Kantees.

She had vowed to save Jelamie, even if it was only a promise to herself. She had promised Welyn she would save his daughter if she could. Or have her revenge. He had not asked for that but she would not leave any of these men alive if it was within her power to bring about their deaths. She had no love for Lorima Hamalain, but they had killed him in cold blood. And these men had shot their own soldier to make sure he could not reveal their secrets.

On the night everything changed.

If it had not happened she would still be in the eyrie at Jakalain with Sheesha, preparing him for the races while dodging Daybian's advances. Something that she would not have been able to do forever. Eventually he would have lost his patience and forced her. But now, she would never be able to do it again. Ever. Was this better or worse? Or was it just different?

But something inside her said that he wouldn't have forced her. It was what he had said himself. If she did not want it, but let him anyway, he did not want it. She would probably have given it to him out of pity. He was not bad for a Taymalin master. Even if he was arrogant. She smiled. It turned out that he had been good with his weapon after all. It had been a very different Daybian fighting in the cavern. A man that she might respect.

Perhaps when she rescued him she would apologise. And he would wonder what for, and she would tell him all the nasty thoughts she had had about him. And he would laugh, because it would be all about him. She changed her mind; apologising to him was a very bad idea.

Sheesha flattened out at a height that gave them a clear view of the coastline and a good distance inland. They could see perhaps seven or eight leagues in all directions. It was invigorating. Out to sea she could see a fishing vessel and wondered if it was the same one as yesterday. If it was, it might give her some idea of how far Sheesha had travelled in that short time. But it might not be.

She allowed her gaze to wander to the coastline ahead of them. It reminded her of a broken biscuit from which bites had been taken at intervals—large and small—and the crumbs scattered in trails out into the ocean. Further along the coast she could see much larger dark lumps curving out from the cliffs and ending in a much larger landmass.

The world was big, she thought, and there was so much to know. She had no idea what those islands were called. Up until a moment ago she had not even known they existed. Did people live on them? If they did, were they free Kadralin? Or Taymalin? Or perhaps even *shocalin*. Did *shocalin* live on land, or only at sea? Did they make their homes inside giant urchins? Of course, that assumed she was right about the creatures she saw being *shocalin* and that they were living inside the shell.

She shook her head. There were more questions in this world than there were answers. She could never know it all. Whether it was about the world around her or the world within. More questions than she knew how to answer.

The afternoon wore on and she ran out of thoughts. She did not have to keep her eyes on the coast the whole time. It seemed to move so slowly she could just glance at it now and then. They passed a dozen tiny fishing villages crowding the cliffs as the mountains closed in tighter to the sea. The cliffs themselves became taller.

They needed to stop. The *ziri* needed to eat. She scanned the coast carefully. Out of the high hills rushed a huge waterfall. The river had created a lake at the top of the cliff but its water leaked down through the rock itself and sprayed out into the sea.

Buildings huddled on the heights, and there were small boats on the lake instead of the ocean. Herds of *fenichasa* and other animals were dotted about chewing on the greenery. She contemplated moving on to a place where they would not be observed but the day was growing late and after their recent experience she thought perhaps they might not be in danger.

At a touch from her knee, Sheesha curved inland and lost height.

She wondered whether she should have consulted with Yenteel but it was almost impossible to have a conversation when flying, and the *zirichasa* seemed disinclined to fly out of their formation. She looked over her shoulder at Yenteel and pointed at the lake. He smiled, so she guessed he thought it was a reasonable decision.

The *ziri* were flying directly at the houses at considerable speed when Kantees realised she might have made a mistake. They had been spotted by somebody and now people were running back and forth among the buildings. Moments later one man with a bow appeared, then another behind him.

Kantees leaned hard to the right and Sheesha veered off. But *Kisharuk* curse her if she was going to let them be forced away by ignorant villagers whose first response was to attack. She kept Sheesha turning until he went into a landing spiral.

They touched down near the drop-off between the cliff and the lake. The ground trembled beneath her feet when she jumped down. A small stream of water ran through what looked like an old riverbed, overgrown with plants. The lake itself had a maelstrom at this end where water fed down into the tunnel below and out from the cliff. The vibration in the ground must be the river forcing its way through the rock.

At the far end of the lake, where the water tumbled from the mountains, a mist filled the air. It was a beautiful place, she thought, except for the men with weapons hurrying in their direction.

"I'll do the talking," said Yenteel.

"Just as you like," she said. "But, to be clear, I do not want to be killed. So don't aggravate them. I came down here because this looked like a good place to feed the *ziri*."

Yenteel did not acknowledge her but walked towards the men with his hands held out to show he was not armed. They did not look friendly.

"Get back on Looesa, Gally," she said. "I am not sure these people will be friends."

"Sheesha wants to eat a *fenichak*," he said.

She stared at him. With everything that had been happening she wondered whether he had learnt how to read their minds. Not that that seemed likely. It wasn't hard to know what a *zirichak* wanted: a place to sleep, a chance to fly fast, and food. They were often fed *fenichasa*, so to their thinking the ones around here were a likely meal.

Her choice of landing place was looking worse by the minute.

She looked across at Yenteel. She couldn't hear what they were saying but the men had lowered their weapons and were talking. At least that meant they weren't going to get shot. Not yet, anyway.

She turned and walked towards the cliff. The grass went right to the edge but she wasn't intending to go too close. It might be treacherous. Then Sheesha's wing came down in front of her and his head curved round as he tried to look at her with both eyes. She smiled at him.

"I wasn't going to jump, Sheesha," she said. "Not this time."

He made a grumbling noise in the back of his very long and deep throat. She leaned against his wing and looked out to sea. There were islands down there. Not big ones, but even the smallest was covered with trees and undergrowth.

"I bet there's food you can eat on those islands, Sheesha." She pointed. "Why don't you have a look? These villagers are too scared of you eating theirs."

And Sheesha looked where she was pointing. He snorted and launched himself off the cliff in a long glide, followed by Shingul. She turned to see why Looesa hadn't gone too but Gally was on his back.

"You can get down, Gally. Looesa can go with Sheesha to get some food."

As Gally slid from the *ziri*'s back, Looesa made a very ungainly run at the cliff edge and launched himself off. For all they were awkward on land, the *zirichasa* were beautiful as they swooped across the intervening water and circled the first of the islands.

"Kantees!"

She tore her eyes from the *ziri* and saw Yenteel beckoning to her. She walked over, not in a hurry, as she had no real interest in what these people had to say.

"This is Bolda," he said indicating the middle-aged man with the bow who stood in front of the others. The men were of various ages, young and old. All looked stern—apart from the youngest who was eyeing her the way young men often did, with his eyes directed at her chest instead of her face. She was used to it.

"Bolda wants to know what you did with the *zirichasa*."

"I sent them to the islands down there to feed," she said to Yenteel, and then addressed Bolda directly. "I guessed you were concerned for your herds."

"You *sent* them?" he said.

"I suggested it."

"You talk to the *ziri*?"

Kantees shrugged. She wasn't going to explain that it wasn't like that. She said things and sometimes Sheesha understood what she wanted, and sometimes he didn't. Let them think she could make herself understood all the time.

"They were hungry and needed to feed."

"Will they come back?"

"Of course."

"We have children here."

"They don't eat children." Wild ones *might* if they were hungry, she supposed, but Kantees was reasonably sure that Sheesha wouldn't. "Especially if they've just eaten."

Yenteel interrupted. "Bolda knows something about the *tekrak*."

"You've seen it?"

"It's one of the reasons they were cautious about us," said Yenteel.

"The man can speak for himself, can't he?" She looked pointedly at Bolda.

"The monstrous thing flew over at midday."

"Which way was it going?"

Bolda pointed further along the coast.

"At midday?" She looked at the position of the sun, behind the light cloud. "We can't be far behind it."

She almost wished she hadn't sent the *ziri* to feed. If she had known before, they could have mounted up and gone after it.

"Why do you seek it?" said Bolda in a cautious voice that almost suggested he didn't want to know.

"They have kidnapped and most likely despoiled children, destroyed one village we know about, and have murdered. I intend to have revenge upon them." She said it in a matter-of-fact way, which was the only way she knew how to deal with what they had done without letting out the anger she held in her heart.

"Did they murder your kin, Mother?"

Kantees hesitated both at the question and his choice of honorific for her. "No, not my kin."

"But you declare a blood feud?"

Was that what it was? She nodded. "It must be done."

"Their crimes are against both Kadralin and Taymalin," said Yenteel. "There are no others who would stand for both, save for Kantees who commands the *zirichasa*."

Her heart froze at Yenteel's words. What pattern was he weaving? Was he attempting to trap her in a legend? Trying to make her into something she wasn't?

She wanted to deny it and make him take the words back, but it was too late. She could see it in the eyes of the men who stood there, see the idea take hold and worm into their minds. She could almost see the way she grew in their eyes—or perhaps it was the way they shrank. Before they had been defiant and willing to fight or even kill her to protect what was theirs. But Yenteel had made them slaves to an idea.

There was nothing she could do now. She would deal with these raiders and then she would turn her back on Yenteel. If she chose to leave there was nothing he could do to stop her. That would stop him doing any more harm. These people did not need someone else to become slave to. There was too much of that already in the world.

They were all looking at her as if they expected something. She glanced at Yenteel, and she could almost see his grin although his face showed nothing of it. It wasn't on the outside but he was triumphant within.

"We need to rest," she said finally. "But have to remain here so the *ziri* know where to find us when they return. And then we'll leave."

"I will send someone with food and water," said Bolda.

She knew better than to insult him by refusing. The group turned away but left two guards.

Kantees lay down on the grass and closed her eyes. She wanted to shout at Yenteel but it would have to wait. He settled himself cross-legged facing her not too far away.

"I hate you," she said in a conversational tone that she did not think would carry to the villagers on guard. "You people say that you only follow the World's Pattern, but the truth is that you bind the world to your own will. You twist it into the image you want."

"I won't deny it."

"Good."

"But that's not the whole story. My master is working for a future for us all."

She propped herself up on her elbows. "What about my choice, Yenteel? What if I don't want this future your master envisages?"

"Then you will prevent it from happening."

"I don't have that sort of power." She lay back again and stared at the mottled cloud shapes above her. She was glad the sun wasn't shining. It would annoy her on a day as depressing as this.

"Power is a strange and fickle thing," he said. "Sometimes it's just a matter of saying the right words at the right moment. Those who try to grab power find it impossible to hold, and it slips through their fingers. Their mistake is in thinking power is something that can be taken. That's not how it is. The Hamalain—even the Jakalain who are less tyrannical—their power is maintained only by force. It is easy for them to lose it, should they slip for only a moment."

"You're going to tell me what it *is* like, I suppose?"

"True power is in giving. It is the willingness to give."

"So you manipulate these poor people into thinking I am some sort of goddess who they can worship and follow?"

"A nudge in the right direction. There may come a time when you need all the help you can get."

Kantees stood up and walked away from him. She went back to the cliff edge and stared out and down at the islands. She couldn't see

Sheesha or the others but that probably meant they were on the ground, eating.

She looked up at the sun again. Time was getting on and they needed to get moving. But the *ziri* would need time to digest before they could move on again.

And they needed a plan.

31

"I want one of your children," said Kantees to Bolda as she ate some of the food the villagers had brought. More fish, naturally, but this time with *kilikash* mashed up on the side melted with *fenichak* cheese. She was surprised how good it was. The *ziri* had returned and were resting while they digested their meal.

Bolda frowned at the question, thinking the worst. Kantees hoped her idea might help to dissipate those Yenteel had planted earlier.

"Why?"

"The child needs to be brave and small to enter the camp of the raiders. They don't have to *be* young but should *look* young. And preferably I'd like a girl."

"But why, Mother?"

Kantees cursed inwardly; this was having the reverse effect because she was asking for something outrageous.

"Ulina," said one of the other men, sitting behind Bolda. "She is crazy and has no family."

Bolda liked that idea. He nodded and the man who had spoken jumped to his feet and went back towards the village.

"What do you mean, crazy?"

"She climbs where no one who valued their life would climb," said Bolda. He pointed at the cliff. "She went down to the sea there because she had found the eggs of a nesting bird on the edge and dropped one."

"But it would be broken," said Kantees.

Bolda shrugged. "She would not say why. But she went down and returned." Then he pointed behind himself at the waterfall that thundered from the mountains. "She climbed to the valley from which the water pours."

Kantees stared. It was higher than a Ziri Tower. "Did she say why she did it?"

"Because she wanted to see."

The conversation lapsed as she, Yenteel, and Gally finished the food that had been brought. She thought she might need a rest to digest the *kilikash*, which now sat heavily on her stomach. It had been good, though. She said so and that pleased Bolda more than it should.

The girl arrived at a run. She was dressed in a smock that had been sewn and patched so much it seemed most of the original material had been replaced. And it was dirty, as were her bare feet. Under the dirt and ragged shift she was pale as any Taymalin and so thin she might have been a spirit barely occupying physical form.

"I am Ulina, Mother, and I would like to ride the *ziri*."

Something about her and the way she spoke made Kantees smile.

"Greetings, Ulina. If you want to ride the *ziri* then you must call me Kantees."

"Why?"

"Because that is my name."

If Kantees had been concerned as to whether Ulina would be as clever as she needed the child to be, that worry was blown away by the quick, brown eyes that took in everything. "You have three *ziri* and there are three of you. What will I ride?"

"You will ride Sheesha with me."

"Then I can go." It was not a question.

Kantees laughed. "Yes, it seems you can. But this will be dangerous and you may be killed. We may all be killed before the sun sets tomorrow."

Now came Ulina's turn to laugh. "Every day we may die. I do not fear death."

"But do you welcome it into your heart?"

"I do not! Because each day is new and there are new things in it. I want to see everything."

Kantees stood up. "Very well, Ulina, I will accept you on this journey, and when it is done you can come back and tell everyone what happened."

"No."

"No?"

"I don't want to come back. I have discovered everything there is to know about this place. I want to see new things. I will only come if you will take me with you forever, Kantees of the *Ziri*."

Kantees looked at Yenteel, who was sitting nearby. Not only had his words worked their patterning on the mind of Bolda and probably those of his men, but it had already spread to the village.

He raised his eyebrows and smiled. "There is nothing more powerful than ideas, Kantees. They burn like fire through wheat fields. And they cannot be extinguished."

"But they can be lost and forgotten, Yenteel," she said and turned back to Ulina. "I promise that I will take you with me, Ulina, until you grow bored with me, or one or other of us is dead."

"Blood bond!" said Ulina. Kantees sighed. Her palm was still tight from where she had cut it to make the paste for the patterning back in the forest. Perhaps she could get away with a small cut on the thumb in this case.

She knelt and pulled out her knife. It was none too sharp after all the use it had had and needed some time with a sharpening block. But Ulina plunged her hand into the neck of her smock and pulled on the chain that hung there until out came a tiny sheath from which she drew a tiny blade.

There were patterns on its surface.

Kantees was aware of these patterned knives but had never seen one; it could cut steel and never needed sharpening. They were worth a thousand slaves. She wondered what the child was doing with it and looked at Bolda, who shrugged.

"She had it with her when she wandered into the village." He gave the impression he wasn't telling the entire truth. But it didn't matter, it explained why they were happy for her to go on this trip. She wasn't really one of theirs.

Kantees pricked her thumb so a drop of blood oozed from it. She handed the tiny blade, shorter than her little finger, back to Ulina who did the same and they pressed their thumbs together.

"There," said Ulina. "Now you must keep your promise."

"I would have anyway."

But Ulina ignored that and put her blade away.

"How old are you?" said Kantees. The girl looked to have perhaps seven or eight years but she seemed older. Ulina shook her head.

"She was three years at most when she turned up here. That was seven years ago."

"Seven boring years," said Ulina.

"Better you take her," said Bolda, "or one day she will anger someone too much. As it is she will die an old maid."

Kantees turned her back on them and went to the *ziri*. She stroked along Sheesha's neck feathers, blue and gold. He was beautiful. And he didn't argue the way people did. The way *she* did.

"Are you ready?" she said.

In response, Sheesha pushed back onto his hind legs, stretched his wings to their full extent, and pushed his head into the sky. He relaxed and shook his feathers back into position. He was ready.

Kantees looked over her shoulder. "Time to go."

If this worked the way she hoped, they would find the *tekrak* on the ground and would be able to put her plan into action. Ulina wasn't vital to the plan but it would help if she could do what was asked of her. Kantees was sure she would at least be willing to try.

Ulina appeared at Kantees' hip, looking up at Sheesha's head and neck.

"He's big."

"He could eat you in one swallow."

"Then I would not be able to come with you."

"But you would be with me. In his tummy."

Without being asked, Sheesha put his head and neck down so Kantees could mount.

"Sheesha, this is Ulina, she's going to be riding with me."

Sheesha grumbled.

"What did he say, Kantees of the *Ziri*?" said Ulina.

"He said he is very strong and won't even notice you."

Kantees put her leg over the *ziri*'s neck, then lifted Ulina up and in front of her. There was a little adjustment to be done but Ulina was so small she could sit between Kantees' legs and still be partly on the wings.

"You can hold on to his feathers," said Kantees. "But don't pull them hard. He won't like it and they will just come out anyway."

With that she gave Sheesha a little squeeze with her thighs. He went back on his haunches and launched himself upwards. Kantees realised she had forgotten to check on the others but a quick glance showed her both Gally and Yenteel were with them.

Ulina laughed as each wingbeat lifted them higher. Kantees turned the *ziri* along the coast and he kept climbing.

"Keep your eyes open for the *tekrak* on the ground, Ulina."

"I will."

The clouds had cleared and, in the east, the mountains were bright against the darkening sky. Kantees was not sure what she was feeling as they travelled along the coast again with the sun descending into the sea. She was excited they would finally catch up with the raiders, but the excitement was mixed with dread and apprehension.

Without Daybian it would be just her and Yenteel against so many armed men. She thought she knew what she needed to do but it depended on many things she did not know, or could only guess.

The sky darkened as the sun burned into the horizon. She hoped that the moons would not appear too soon. They needed as much dark as possible.

Stars emerged as the sky went black and still they flew. The temperature dropped. Kantees put her arms around Ulina, partly to keep the girl warm but also to stay warm herself.

The *ziri* were not bothered by the dark, just as she thought. It was always assumed they wanted to sleep at night because that's what their owners and keepers did. The *zirichasa* were happy to oblige but it seemed night-time sleep was not a requirement.

The sea was one shade of dark, reflecting the stars, but the land was a deeper dark with the occasional fire, or houses lit from the inside.

"Kantees of the Ziri," said Ulina, and she pointed.

Kantees followed the direction the child was pointing and saw the open campfires highlighting the great round body of the *tekrak*. Her heart jumped, her breathing quickened, and fear crept through her fingers.

The time had come.

32

Bright Lostimal had stayed below the horizon so far but Colimar had risen, casting its wan red light across the land. Perhaps it was for the best; they needed some light, but not too much.

Kantees and Gally stood with the three *ziri* on the edge of the cliff. From below the breaking waves roared their constant thunder. Yenteel and Ulina were making their way inland towards a low ridge. The raiders' encampment was out of sight over the top.

They had doubled back a good distance and then flown in low across the sea, finally rising up to land at the top without being seen in the dim red moonlight. That part of the plan had gone well enough, but there was nothing to disrupt it. If Ulina failed, the raiders would be on their guard.

"But what if they stay awake all night?" Kantees had said to Yenteel.

"They are arrogant men and they have alcohol," he replied. "They will drink themselves into a stupor."

"They will have men on guard."

"Who will also be drinking, because they are raiders and mercenaries who have no paymaster but themselves."

"They will be wreaking their lusts on the girls."

Yenteel could not deny it. "That is why we are here, Kantees. We cannot save them from the past, but we can save them from the future."

And he had said it in such a pointed way that she could not help but think of his words about his master, and her. In what way was her interference any different from someone who wanted to save the world?

She did not want to save the world—just the girls. She had seen plenty who were mistreated, women of any age who bore the marks of men who owned them in one way or another. It was not fair and those that did it should be punished.

But she was risking the lives of Yenteel, Ulina, and Gally just to do it. Did she have that right? Ulina certainly didn't understand.

So she had tried to explain.

"My master told me to obey your instructions," said Yenteel.

"Even to death?" She had become exasperated with his attitude.

"He did say it could happen, but then nothing in this world is certain, Kantees. I could be eaten by a wild *zirichak* tomorrow." Then he smiled, and she wanted to hit him.

"It's an adventure," said Ulina. "Today I flew higher than anything I could climb and saw the world."

"But the raiders will hurt you if you are caught."

"Any pain will be theirs."

Kantees gave up. She needed them for this to work the best way that it could. Without them, it was doubtful she could succeed at all.

But after they had gone, it was Gally who was her biggest problem.

"Gally will go with Kantees."

She did not know what to say. She did not simply want to forbid him because it did not seem the decent thing to do. She wanted him to at least understand enough to make the decision himself.

"I must make the golden flower with Sheesha, Gally." She did not know if the others could do it. And as it was, she would be asking Sheesha to do something so very dangerous she might kill them both before they even reached the raiders. "You must stay here with Looesa and Shingul so they are here when Yenteel and Ulina return."

"Gally knows all die, maybe."

She sighed. "Yes. We may not come back."

"Gally knows you must do the good thing."

She smiled with tears in her eyes.

"You have enough food to stay here two nights, Gally. If no one has come you can fly back to the burned village and stay with them. Lintha will look after you."

"Yenteel likes Lintha."

"He does. And Lintha will be sad if we don't come back. But Gally, stay two nights and then go to Lintha. You understand?"

"Gally knows."

And that was the best she could do.

She looked up at Colimar. Yenteel was knowledgeable about the stars as well and he gave her instructions. And the time had come.

She gave Gally a kiss on his cheek. "I will return as soon as I can."

"Goodbye, Kantees of the Ziri."

She suppressed her frown and did not tell him off for using the name. She wanted him to be as happy as possible.

Now she was hoping Looesa and Shingul did not get it into their heads to follow Sheesha. They had no reins or tethers, so there was nothing Gally could do to stop them, but it would spoil everything if they did.

Thankfully, as she urged Sheesha into the air, the other two remained on the ground.

She had Sheesha dip down to the sea so they would not be observed, and only started him into a climb when they were a good distance out. It was strange, she thought, how she never felt unsafe when she was on his back, even though she had no saddle and no buckles. Riding this way seemed natural.

As he spiralled up, she saw the raiders' camp. The fires were lower now. She thought she could hear singing—raucous and tuneless. It was pierced by a child's scream. She shivered as it penetrated her heart like a knife. What if that was Ulina? They would not hesitate to torture her.

And even if it wasn't her, it could be Jakanda, or one of the others.

She must stay with the plan. But what if Yenteel had been captured too?

On the next of Sheesha's spiral turns the camp looked different, as if it was fading out. The fires were blurred and indistinct. On the next turn it was clear the mist had risen. Yenteel had not been captured; he had used the first of Lintha's patterns. Now that the mist was firmly in place, it was as if it had a long tail that stretched from the camp all the way to the cliff and down into the sea. It wasn't localised around the camp but spread out in the valley, filling it up to the ridges on either side and spilling over.

That was her signal.

Without another word from her, Sheesha dived. She leaned forwards onto his neck and wrapped her arms around it. This was the third time and she was used to it, and she even felt a confident calm from Sheesha himself.

The magic within him boiled up and overflowed. This time she tried to stay in control, not just be a passenger. The golden glow flowed around them. Sheesha's wings folded back. She aimed at the river of mist. It took the merest fraction of time and they were into it.

The mist around them glowed with gold while silence still enfolded them. Half a heartbeat later they shot back out into the night.

Sheesha slowed immediately and his wings flashed out to beat against the sudden blast of wind as they came to a halt. He spun in the air.

It was as if a knife had sliced through the mist and torn it apart along its length. The top and side of the *tekrak* had been exposed. Yenteel should have stopped the pattern but it would take a while for the mist to dissipate, if it did at all.

With the magic gone, she could hear uproar in the camp but could see very little. Until a raider came running from the mist, screaming in terror. He shouted something about demons and magic. Then he looked up to see Sheesha. And he saw his death.

Kantees jumped from his back. It was a longer drop than she expected, and she fell heavily on her ankle and collapsed to the floor. Sheesha dropped like a stone onto the raider and cut his scream short.

She got to her feet. Her ankle was not broken but perhaps a little sprained, so she hobbled forwards. Two men came from the mist just in time to see their compatriot ripped in half.

Their shock at the sight was short-lived as Sheesha pounced. His long neck snaked out and snapped at the head of one while he brought his tail round and knocked the second off his feet and then stomped him with a hind leg and crushed him with a talon.

The mist was clearing faster than Kantees expected. Perhaps the magic was the only thing holding it in place. She desperately wanted to know if Ulina had managed to get the children free but she dared not call out.

The noise in the place was increasing. Lostimal, as Yenteel had said it would, was lifting behind the mountains and light was growing.

She wanted to kill all the raiders but right now she would be glad to be gone from there. She could not fight.

"Who are you?"

The speaker was a man in need of a shave and missing half his clothes but he seemed comfortable with the sword in one hand and the knife in the other.

Strands of mist wove in and out of the bushes and trees as if they did not want to leave. They took turns hiding and revealing the man as he walked towards her.

He took in her simple clothes and grinned. "Never mind. It doesn't matter who you are, your pattern ends here."

Kantees heard a movement behind her. The man stopped and his eyes went up.

"You need to know my name, so you can tell whatever demon claims your pattern what it was that killed you," she said. "I am Kantees of the Ziri, and I will have revenge on you in the name of those you have hurt."

Sheesha roared. It was less thunderous than it had been underground, but frightening nonetheless.

"So, raider, murderer, ravisher of children, who are you?"

"I am Ofindah, captain of armsmen, and slayer of Kantees."

He moved in a relaxed motion, bringing his arm up swiftly and releasing the dagger from his hand. She blinked. Everything happened in slow motion. She wanted to get out of the way, but Sheesha was behind her and she dared not move in case he was hurt.

The blade struck her in the shoulder, and for a moment she thought he must have thrown badly. Then the pain flashed through her and she went down on one knee with the shock of it.

"So much for your revenge, Kantees of the Ziri."

A child screamed but it was not a scream of pain. Ulina materialised from the curling mists and climbed the man like a tree. Her tiny patterned knife sliced across the side of his neck. He shrugged her off as if he had not felt the injury—just as Kantees had not felt hers—and Ulina landed hard with a cry that *was* of pain.

Kantees leaned against Sheesha's wing and forced herself back onto her feet.

In Ofindah's eyes she saw the realisation that something was not right. He raised his hand to his neck and touched it. The shadows meant Kantees could not see clearly, but he brought his hand back and stared at the fingers.

She could feel the dagger grating against her bones as she staggered forwards. The pain kept her focused.

The raider swayed but still clung to his sword and raised it as she approached. She ignored it.

"Do you feel it, Ofindah?" she said. "Your pattern being rubbed out?"

He opened his mouth as if to speak but only blood spilled from it. His eyes glazed over.

Despite the pain, she forced herself to remain standing so that her face would be the very last thing he saw. The sword slipped from his fingers and clattered to the ground. His eyes rolled up into his head and he crumpled.

Kantees did not feel at all well. Her legs went weak and she fell to her hands and knees.

I cannot stop now, she thought. *That's only one.*

Someone small got under her arm and helped her stay on her feet. Ulina.

The bulk of the *tekrak* loomed to Kantees' left. In the light of Lostimal she could make out its great curved roots digging into the soil. It did not have the basket under it; they must remove it at night.

She staggered forwards again with Ulina at her side and Sheesha at her back. A man came running from the mist, saw her, and then looked up at the *ziri*. He fled the way he had come. Another *ziri* roar came from in front of them.

Looesa and Shingul had not stayed put. Gally would be upset.

The mist ahead glowed red with a fire's embers.

"The carriage, Ulina?" Her words did not seem very clear.

"I got the others out," said the child. "Like you told me."

"Jelamie?"

"Only peasant children, Kantees of the Ziri."

"Don't," she said, but could not get the rest of the words out. Ulina would not understand what she was talking about. She desperately wanted to pull the dagger from her shoulder but she knew that could make the wound worse. She could bleed like Ofindah until she had lost so much blood she would die of it. *Jelamie?*

She had made a promise to herself. She had told her promise to Daybian. She would find his brother.

If he still lived.

The sounds of men screaming and dying had stopped now. And as they made their way through the mists, they saw nothing to tell them many men had died. She hoped they were all dead. She hoped they had all suffered and had been terrified in their last moments. She wanted them to have understood what their victims had suffered.

She heard a sob. At first it sounded like one of the dying men, but when it came again she knew it was someone young. Ulina had said the villagers' children had been freed, hadn't she? Kantees was having trouble concentrating. The pain distracted her.

The sound seemed to come from the *tekrak*, now behind her.

She tried to say the boy's name but her voice did not seem to want to work anymore. It was almost as if she was too tired to speak. So instead she forced herself to go back, which confused both her companions. Then Ulina must have heard it too, because she almost dragged Kantees towards the sound.

The fire-tube of the huge flying plant was as broad as Ulina was high. The silver light of Lostimal gleamed off its curved surface. The ridges of the leaves from which it was composed were shadowy lines.

She could smell the noxious gas the *tekrak*'s body contained as it leaked between the leaves.

A small foot hung from the tube.

When Kantees reached out to touch it, it was pulled in immediately.

Kantees concentrated on her throat. "Jelamie," she croaked. "It's Kantees, from Jakalain."

The boy wailed.

33

The patterner had been found hiding behind a chest in the carriage. He had been as mistreated as the rest but perhaps, as an adult, he could make more sense of it.

Yenteel had come down when the fighting had stopped and he was sure the *ziri* had won. He made no pretence of bravery but put his limited healing skills to work on Kantees' injury. She kept Ofindah's knife on her belt, in the sheath she had taken from his dead body.

They would not bury or burn the dead raiders, but rather would leave them to the elements and the animals. There were too many anyway, and they deserved no such respect.

Three of the children, Jelamie among them, did not say anything but stared with wild eyes at the *ziri*. The patterner would not talk about what had happened. He just shook his head when Kantees asked. But he did explain the boy had not been the target of the raid; that was his elder brother, and they had not even known Jelamie was aboard until late the following day. After they had killed Lorima Hamalain. The patterner either did as he was told or he would suffer. He chose to obey.

The raiders had decided to keep Jelamie as a pet—though they mistreated him and forced him to sleep in the *tekrak*'s fire-tube. It amused them, seeing him trying to rest with the fear that if he over-slept he might be incinerated.

As dawn approached, the patterner spoke to Kantees. She was very tired but had found it impossible to sleep.

"I will lose the *tekrak*," he said. "Unless we can move it over to the carriage."

"I don't understand."

"When the sun shines on its leaves, it will ignite its fire-tube and take off. We have to move it to the carriage where I can make it wrap its roots around the structure. Then it will obey."

"Why not let it go?" Then she stopped and with her good hand grabbed him by the collar. "Where did you get this monster and how did you learn to control it?"

He shut his mouth and looked at her in fear, as if she were one of the raiders. Her shoulder ached and she knew she was just tired. She released him.

The glow of dawn was lighting the sky behind the mountains. She could simply release the *tekrak* but then they would be many people and just three *ziri*. Or she could let this man control it and they could all ride. He knew things she needed to know—perhaps where they had taken Daybian, or at least a clue she could follow.

"Very well. What must we do?"

She put Ulina in charge of the girls and Jelamie with instructions to clear out the carriage of anything they did not need. She had taken a look inside and concluded it was a disgusting mess. The patterner explained how the glyphs for control were etched into the roof of the carriage itself, but that meant the *tekrak* must be manhandled into position. Once in place, it would not let go until the magic was released.

It took many of the raiders to hold the monster down each morning while they moved it. Now they had three humans and three *ziri*. Kantees was not sure how Sheesha and the others would feel about holding ropes.

She set Gally to making loops in the cords that hung from the net thrown across the *tekrak*'s body. The net itself was not tied to the crea-ture but she needed no explanation for that. Leaving aside the risk of puncturing its body, the net stretched as it strained. There was no way of holding it in place.

She went to the elongated front of the monster. It was hard to understand how it could navigate without eyes or ears, or even a sense of smell. But it did: probably another manifestation of its magic.

Sheesha came willingly when she called to him, and at her word Looesa and Shingul came too. She had noticed how they followed Sheesha's lead and copied what he did, so she wanted them to watch —hoping only that Sheesha did not protest.

The *ziri* wore their tack easily enough but that was what they were trained for. This would be different. There had not been time to be clever. She had Sheesha duck his head and she slipped the loop over it, then brought it down his neck to his body. His wings were partly spread because he had used them to walk over.

Kantees pushed him down so he was lying prone. He turned his long neck to watch what she was doing. He was biddable and trusting, but curious. She hoped she was not about to betray that trust.

Now that he was prone, he automatically brought his wings in next to his body. Kantees only wanted the loop to go over one of them, but she made it as big as she could. She glanced again at the sky. The sun would be here soon. She pushed the loop back along his body on one side and, pulling hard, managed to get it over the hooks and claws of the wing's leading edge, just as Sheesha thought she was trying to get him to stand again.

His wings stretched and the loop lay diagonally across his body. He pulled at it experimentally.

"Just wait, Sheesha," she said with an outward calm she was not feeling inside. "Wait. Let's get the others into theirs, shall we?"

She went to the side of the huge *tekrak* and called to Shingul while Gally led Looesa round the other way. As she had expected, Shingul was a little jumpier and kept looking at Sheesha, but he remained calm so she did, too. Kantees went through the same process, which was easier the second time—and perhaps because Shingul was smaller.

When she was done, Kantees ran to where Gally was working, only to find that he had already succeeded. Both he and Looesa had smug looks. She laughed, then jumped as the *tekrak* creaked. She spun around. The roots were coming out of the ground. They had been barely in time with the ropes.

But now was the real test.

She hurried back to Sheesha in case he needed calming, but he was merely watching the movement of the plant with half an eye. Quite disinterested. She supposed this might be because it wasn't edible.

But, as the roots came up, the great green ball of leaves creaked again and lifted. Gally and Yenteel had been assigned ropes at the far end, near the fire-tube but not in line with it. Kantees did not have a rope but she thought she might be able to push from this side. She wanted to be able to see everything and guide them. Or calm the *ziri* if that was needed.

She worried about what might happen if one of them panicked and decided the rope was a trap. This was a tremendously dangerous thing they were doing. The *ziri* could hurt themselves, or hurt someone else. Men could understand—the *zirichasa* simply trusted. And it was her they put their faith in.

She saw light under the *tekrak*. The biggest roots had drawn up, with soil and plants dripping from them like water. The ropes and net stretched. Soon there was enough space for the children to go under it, though they were standing off to the side and watching with no excitement. They had seen this before.

"Gally! Yenteel! Start to walk towards the carriage!" They obeyed easily enough but the *ziri* were not looking happy. The ropes pulling across their bellies was not something they were used to.

"Sheesha," she said in a sharp tone. "Come on." And she started to walk towards the body of the *tekrak* in slow, small steps—it wasn't a great distance but she wanted Sheesha to get the idea they were going somewhere. The big *ziri* grunted and she saw the rope over her head slacken as he moved after her.

"Shingul! Looesa! Move!"

They looked at her. They looked at Sheesha, who grunted again. They hesitated.

"Looesa, go to Gally!" And she pointed. Thankfully *ziri* were brighter than *zatesa,* who were good for guarding and being pets but would have just looked at her pointing finger. Looesa knew who Gally was and turned his head. "Gally, tell him to come. Yenteel, call to Shingul, ask her to come to you."

They did as she said and the *ziri* walked. Luckily, again unlike *zatesa*, they were big and preferred to move slowly—at least on the ground. So they didn't rush.

Kantees breathed a sigh of relief. If it worked now, it could work in the evening. She imagined the horror on Daybian's face if he'd seen this. Using the racing *zirichasa* as beasts of burden! She smiled to herself.

They got the *tekrak* in position and the patterner, in his chair at the front of the carriage, muttered to himself and chanted. The roots came alive once more and wound themselves around the ironwork.

The loose ropes were tied off on stakes already driven into the ground. Otherwise, the carriage would lift. Then Kantees and Gally released the *ziri*. Sheesha proceeded to investigate the plant and its roots as if it had now become something of interest. He even poked his head inside the carriage and sniffed the patterner.

"Gally and Yenteel, you ride in the basket with the children. I will fly with the *ziri*."

"You shouldn't ride the *ziri*, you're just a slave."

Kantees turned and stared at Jelamie. Those were the first words he had spoken. She wanted to be angry with him, but it would not be fair. He was still a child, and he had been sorely used by these men.

Instead she went down on one knee although it hurt her shoulder to do so. Yenteel had only had time to do a simple pattern that mended the worst.

"You would be right, Jelamie, if I were still a slave, but I am not. On the night of the raid I freed myself so that I was able to ring the warning bell and bring out the armsmen to fight the raiders."

He looked confused. The idea that slaves might free themselves did not fit with his understanding. But he was too young see a flaw in the argument. He just felt it was inherently wrong. But for Kantees herself it was a revelation. She had said the words simply to placate him, but the truth of them struck her: She had freed herself because freedom was something you claimed as your right. It could not be given because that validated slavery itself.

"And if I had not freed myself I could not have come on the *ziri* to rescue you."

"You came for me?"

"Of course. What other reason could I have?"

And that, at least, was the complete truth. She decided not to mention that Daybian had also been on the journey. Explaining that his brother was captured and possibly dead would not do the boy any good at all. No, she would not burden him further, and she would tolerate anything unpleasant he said.

"Come on, it's time to go," she said and held out her hand. He hesitated for a moment, then raised his pale fingers to her dark ones. Then he threw himself into her arms, weeping.

Pain shot through her shoulder but she bit down on her lip to keep from crying out. Instead she enfolded him and held him. Her own eyes filled with tears.

First they would take the girls back to their village. That would take a day. Then they would fly the monstrous beast close to Jakalain and she would take Jelamie to his parents, though she would not linger. They would soon have her in irons and destined for the noose if she gave them half a chance—freedom might be claimed but it was easily lost if one was not careful. She would have Yenteel write a letter that Jelamie could deliver explaining the situation.

And then?

Then she would make the patterner tell her what she needed to know and find Daybian.

And after that, Kantees of the Ziri? asked the voice in her head.

"We'll see," she said out loud.

~ End of Book 1 ~

AFTERWORD

If you enjoyed **REBEL DRAGON**, why not write a review on the site you bought it at, or on Goodreads (even both).

The story of Kantees continues in **OUTLAW DRAGON** (taupress.com/outlaw-dragon),

or you can buy all the books in one volume: THE DRAGONS OF ESTERNES (taupress.com/esternes-dragons).